Codename: Starman

Book 3

The God Satellite

Books by Mack Maloney

Mack Maloney's Haunted Universe
Iron Star
Thunder Alley

Wingman *series*
The Odessa Raid
Battle of the Wingmen
The Jericho Storm

Codename: Starman *series*
The Kalashnikov Kiss
The Sea of Moons
The God Satellite

Starhawk *series*
Starhawk
Planet America
The Fourth Empire
Battle at Zero Point
Storm Over Saturn

Chopper Ops *series*
Chopper Ops
Zero Red
Shuttle Down

Strikemasters *series*
Strikemasters
Rogue War
Fulcrum

Storm Birds *series*
Desert Lightning
Thunder from Heaven
The Gathering Storm

Codename: Starman

Book 3

The God Satellite

Mack Maloney

SPEAKING VOLUMES, LLC
NAPLES, FLORIDA
2022

The God Satellite

ISBN 978-1-64540-740-9

Codename: Starman

Book 3

The God Satellite

Mack Maloney

SPEAKING VOLUMES, LLC
NAPLES, FLORIDA
2022

The God Satellite

ISBN 978-1-64540-740-9

For the Entire MMMX-Files Gang

Part One

<u>One of Our Tomato Cans is Missing</u>

Chapter One

This is how it happened:

Father Fred Friendly, ex-U.S. Navy SEAL chaplain, walked into the Encore Casino in Boston with $20,000, won $800,000 at roulette, won another $9.5 *million* at an illegal high-stakes poker game and then caught a flight to Ireland, all in a matter of a few hours.

He died at the end of a quixotic quest to give his winnings to disadvantaged war victims in Northern Ireland, keeping with him the secret of how he won all that money so quickly in the first place.

Until now.

Special Agent Maura McCann was sitting at Angel's kitchen table, drinking a cup of tea.

She was in her mid-20s, five-four, with dark red hair and incredibly bright blue eyes—they were almost neon. She was wearing a green buttoned-up sweater, a short green tartan skirt, black tights and clogs—the same outfit she wore when Chris Starr first met her a few months ago. And just like then, she was looking at him now with a gigantic smile.

Maura was an investigator for Ireland's Special Detective Service, part of the Irish National Police. Starr was a special agent for NILE, as in U.S. Naval Intelligence Law Enforcement. Together not only had they pursued Father Friendly during his bizarre journey through Ireland, they were the last people to see him alive. He practically died in Maura's arms.

But what remained was how someone not known to be a gambler could have been so incredibly lucky to win almost $10 million in no time at all.

"It turns out he wasn't *that* lucky," Maura was saying now. "But nor was he cheating. Not really. I think he had help—from a spy satellite."

Starr took a seat at the table. He and his girlfriend Angel lived together—sort of. Hauntingly gorgeous, Angel was a much in-demand cover model; he was basically a military detective in a unit that took on so many weird cases for the U.S. Navy, they were known as the "The X-Files Guys." They'd found Maura waiting for them in the lobby of their apartment building as they were returning from Starr's most recent assignment.

He'd been quite taken with her during their time together in Eire, but when they'd parted—with a long hug and almost a kiss—he wasn't sure if he'd ever see her again.

Now here she was. In his girlfriend's kitchen, talking about a spy satellite with a gambling problem.

Maura finished her tea. Instead of refilling her cup, Angel asked if she'd like something stronger.

"I'd never say no to that," Maura replied.

Angel opened her refrigerator to reveal one level stacked with high-priced Irish beer. Starr stared at the emerald-bottle array. Angel's fridge rarely held more than a container of fruit and a few bottles of sparkling water.

She got Irish beer? How did she know?

She opened three bottles and passed them around.

"I believe Father Friendly *did* have help from above," Maura continued after her first sip. "Just not the kind we were thinking of. Instead, I think he somehow tapped into a spy satellite so secret I'll bet your fancy Space Force doesn't even know about it. I think this satellite allowed him to not only manipulate things on the floor of that casino, but also gave him 'eyes *and* ears in the room' when he was winning at the illegal poker game later on."

"All that through a satellite?" Starr asked.

"Yes," she replied definitively.

He thought a moment, not wanting to dampen her sunny enthusiasm.

"I can tell you our best spy satellites can count the buttons on your jacket from about a hundred miles up,"

4

he said. "But they can't see inside structures. Or hear inside them. This seems like a stretch."

"That's because your thinking is too linear," Maura replied matter-of-factly.

She looked over at Angel and they both laughed.

Two redheads.

"Such a guy . . ." Angel said.

Starr plunged on.

"Okay," he said. "Then where would a satellite possibly get all the data it would need to do these things, and do them instantaneously?"

"About that, I'm not so sure," Maura admitted, adding. "I have a theory, though . . ."

She took an extra-long sip of beer and then began.

"Our lives are surrounded and saturated by electronic signals," she began. "Audio, video, radio, data-bursts. Signals from electronic bugs, security cameras, cell phones, you name it—they're all invisible, but they're around us every moment of every day.

"I think this satellite can sweep up targeted electronic signals, combine them, digest them, make some sense of them and then spit out an instantaneous result, something that very closely resembles the reality of the moment you want to know about—and at any given moment you want."

Starr was listening intently, trying hard to understand. But the concept was eluding him.

Not so Angel.

"Do you mean like matching security camera footage to the audio of a bugging device?" she asked Maura. "Even though the two might not be necessarily connected?"

"Exactly," Maura told her. "And in today's world, imagine being able to do that on an almost unlimited scale. For example, most Smart-TVs have the ability to spy on their owners. Most people leave their Alexa or Siri turned on which means those little monsters are always eavesdropping on us. I think this satellite can meld things like that together instantly. Eyes and ears in the room. And, as I'll bet it's all run by artificial intelligence—*voila*, we have 'artificial reality.' "

"That's catchy," Angel said.

"There's more," Maura went on. "I think this satellite might also be able to manipulate that reality by hacking into just about any kind of electronic device there is. And *that's* how Father Friendly won all that money. He had this incredible resource floating around up in space at his disposal."

Starr chugged down the rest of his beer, one, two, three gulps and it was gone. This was starting to sound like a James Bond movie and not a particularly good one. His facial expression must have showed as much.

"OK," Maura went on, her tone turning more serious, "just imagine the room where Friendly's card game was held being filled with hidden security cameras. He was playing with some pretty high-level gangsters. The local police, the FBI or maybe even the casino itself could have been looking in on them. Surveillance is everywhere these days.

"By combining all those video signals, I think this satellite could determine what cards were left in the deck and *then* calculate the probability of which ones Father Friendly was going to get. It did the thinking for him, and told him how to play every hand."

"But how could he possibly be in touch with this satellite while he was playing cards," Starr asked. "And with some hoodlums, yet?"

"By using a simple code of transmitted vibrations," Maura told him. "Call them beeps only he could hear. One sequence might mean: play the inside straight. Another might mean stand pat or take four or something. Think of God Himself watching a poker game and knowing what everyone else has and what they're going to do—and then passing that information on to you."

Angel handed Starr another beer.

"That would be a dream come true," he admitted, twisting off the top. "But, remember, Father Friendly won at roulette earlier—and that's completely random. Spin the wheel and the ball drops where the ball drops. And it's not like a big casino like that is going to use electronics to manipulate the wheel or anything. The house always wins, they don't have to cheat."

"All true," Maura said, taking off her sweater to reveal a white blouse beneath, simple and tight. "But that night, Father Friendly played an *electronic* roulette machine. Encore Boston was one of the first big casinos to get them. Basically you put in your chips, push a button and the wheel spins itself, letting the ball 'drop' into a slot after going through billions of possible outcomes and permutations. But I think, thanks to the God Satellite, the good father was able to win because it knew what numbers he bet on and would have them hit accordingly."

Angel reached across the table and gently touched Maura's hand.

"Did you just say the 'God Satellite?' " she asked.

Maura blushed. "It needed a name," she said. "So I came up with 'Geospatial Observation and Data'—GOD. I think it's in a very low orbit meaning it can be directed at a target and stay on it almost indefinitely even as the planet turns. If it's cloudy it goes strictly infrared; at night, same thing with NightVision. Put it all together and it's like God Himself is looking directly down at you."

Angel laughed. "I think it's a great name."

"Right?" Maura said clinking beer bottles with her.

Meanwhile Starr's head was starting to spin. The capabilities Maura claimed this satellite possessed was far beyond any spy technology he'd ever heard of—and he had top clearance from the Navy.

"How did you come up with all this?" he finally asked her.

She'd been waiting for the question. Reaching into her gig bag—which was an oversized and overflowing backpack—she took out a bronze metal box. About seven inches long and half that wide, it looked like a little coffin.

"Because I found this," she said.

She flipped open the lid—and Starr and Angel both gasped.

Inside was a Tomato Can.

It looked like an old, toy walkie-talkie from the 1960s.

Cracked plastic, a thin veneer of black paint flaking away, its screen scratched and scraped. But when you turned it on, this facade slid away to reveal a second device hidden beneath, one with a screen that lit up like the dashboard of a '85 Corvette. Deploy the little dish antenna and you were in business. It was a satellite phone. It could work in any weather, just about anywhere on Earth.

But as cool as they were, this particular model was obsolete—in fact, up until that moment, Starr would have bet he and Angel had the last two working pair on the planet. He'd been issued them the first day he joined NILE, but when newer models became available, no one ever asked him to turn in the old ones. So he gave one to Angel, under the strict condition she use it only in dire emergencies—but that didn't last long. She called him on it all the time, which was a huge security risk, but always just their little secret.

Now for them to see this third one was worthy of a gasp.

Angel said nothing. Trying very hard to look surprised, Starr asked Maura: "What is that thing?"

"I'm certain it's a communication device used in the past by someone's Special Forces . . ." she replied earnestly.

She called up a photo on her cell phone. It showed a wrecked car on the back of a flatbed truck. There was so much damage, it would have been hard to tell what kind of car it was. But Starr recognized it right away. It was the vintage Jaguar Father Friendly had leased for his dash to Northern Ireland. It wound up getting shot up and totaled by the end.

"The Irish judicial system had me inventory this bloody thing," Maura said, "and write up a report—before they had it crushed to scrap and sold to China. But I'm glad I did, because I found this—this little casket—with that thing inside. It was hidden in a plastic cooler under the back seat."

"But it looks like a toy," Starr said, maintaining his poker face.

"Even so, watch this," she said.

She pushed a button on the side and the hidden device below was revealed, looking just like the pair he and Angel had.

"It's really neat camouflage, don't you think?" Maura asked.

Starr and Angel exchanged a quick glance and simultaneous eye-rolls.

"But I believe," Maura went on, "that Father Friendly somehow got ahold of this and that he used it to communicate with the God Satellite. I think he had it in his pocket while playing roulette and during the card game and that the satellite talked to him in silent beeps. That's how he pulled it off."

Starr shifted uneasily in his seat. The priest winning millions thanks to a secret satellite? A satellite that could seemingly do all, know all? Everything Maura was saying sounded too way-out, too fringe-y. But . . . if even a small fraction of it was true, Starr would have to report it to his superiors. That would be a big step, for several reasons, not the least of which was that now, a Tomato Can was involved.

"What proof do we have that this super satellite actually exists?" he asked her, hoping against hope that her answer would be: none.

But Maura was always full of surprises—and as it turned out, she had some interesting data to back up her theory.

She handed Starr a thumb drive.

"It's all on there," she said. "Compliments of my dear Finny."

Maura had a brother back in Dublin named Finny; Starr had met him. He was a brilliant Irish egghead who ran a private satellite tracking firm. Strictly a one-man operation, he was so smart, he could do with spare parts and duct tape what some intelligence agencies spent billions on.

Maura explained that Finny had transferred everything in this third Tomato Can's memory to his own lap top. Then, by distilling that information, he was able to establish that this particular 'Can had been involved in hundreds of satellite transmissions during the time it was in Father Friendly's possession, with constant messages between Earth and orbit, being sent back and forth.

This was especially true during Friendly's strange evening at the Encore Casino. Finny discovered that not only was the poker game being bugged by no less than three different law enforcement entities with a half dozen miniature video cameras and listening devices hidden throughout the suite, there was also a lot of chatter between Friendly and the satellite consisting mostly of short bursts of barely audible buzzers and beeps during the game.

So the priest was definitely up to something that night and using the Tomato Can to do it. But was he really communing with a super-satellite that could create an all-encompassing bubble of artificial reality as Maura described? To know everything, to see everything inside that bubble—in real time, without anyone realizing it?

If true, the personal privacy implications for every person on Earth were enormous. But for military planners and spies, such a weapon would indeed be a God-send of mind-blowing proportions.

The final file on Finny's thumb drive documented how he and Maura had taken *such* a deep dive into the

'Can's satellite data that they'd discovered a flaw in their orbital deity-tabbed system.

For reasons unknown, the God Satellite occasionally took a long time to respond to urgent requests. And sometimes it simply didn't respond at all.

"Just like the real one," Maura said.

***

They stayed at the kitchen table for another hour, drinking more beer and re-reading some of Finny's encrypted thumb-drive documents. Even more the second time around, they told an outlandish, 007-ish tale. But in the end, Starr had to admit, there might be something to it.

When it grew to be almost midnight, Angel and Maura excused themselves and disappeared into Angel's bedroom.

Both were in silk pajamas when they returned; Maura wearing a pair borrowed from Angel's endless clothes' closet.

Clearly exhausted, their guest bid Starr goodnight.

"Next step tomorrow?" she asked him.

"For sure . . ." he said.

She went back to the bedroom, leaving Angel and Starr alone.

"Strange turn of events," Angel half-whispered, hugging him from behind. "What do you think's going on?"

Starr just shrugged. "There might be a chance someone's super-duper secret satellite got hacked," he said. "And she and Finny just stumbled on to it, thanks to Father Friendly."

"But could a satellite really do all those things?" she asked. "All-powerful, all-knowing, possessing manipulative powers, looking down on us from above? I mean, she really nailed it with that name."

"No satellite I know of even comes close," he said. "Sounds more like something from a galaxy far, far away."

She thought a moment then said: "We probably shouldn't have used our 'Cans so much. I feel dumb now for doing it at all. It's going to get you in trouble."

But Starr shook her concerns away.

"I'll worry about that when the time comes," he told her. "Number one problem right now is I *have* to bring this upstairs. And I mean *way* upstairs, so the chances of me making an ass of myself will be significant and great. But I just can't sit on it. If by some chance any of it is true and they found out I knew, they'll ship me to Tonga before I can say *oka-oka al-yu . . .*"

Angel knew what would happen next: he'd be on a flight to Washington, DC, early the next morning; his destination, headquarters for U.S. Naval Intelligence.

"Better get some sleep then," she said, kissing him.

She went into the bedroom while he turned off the lights. When he joined her there, he saw Maura was already under the covers on the bed—and she was on his side.

He looked at Angel, as if to ask: Now what?

She gave him a little push towards her enormous closet.

"Worm hole," she said.

He and Angel actually lived in adjoining apartments at San Diego's Park 12 on Imperial Avenue. Because a co-habitation situation would be problematical at this point in both their careers, he'd cut an elaborate hole in the wall between their units, creating a secret passage-way. The worm hole.

But now, with those two words, he was about to spend the first night in his own apartment in a very long time.

He gave one more look back at Maura, smiling away, and then to Angel as she was climbing in beside her.

"Just make sure you two say your prayers," he said dryly.

Angel gave him a shooing motion and then turned out the light.

Starr went into the closet, parted the way between two stylish Russian wool coats and was suddenly in his own kitchen.

He grabbed one of his own beers, drained it, grabbed another one, drained *it*, then collapsed on his couch and waited for sleep to come.

He was not looking forward to tomorrow.

Chapter Two

The Office of U.S. Naval Intelligence was NILE's higher command.

Their headquarters was located just outside DC, at the National Maritime Intelligence Center in Suitland, Maryland.

It looked more like a college. Made up of four separate sub-commands, it was four interconnected buildings, sizable but also cleverly subdued. But this was the Navy's spy palace, its special ops Taj Mahal—and this would be Starr's first visit here. Everything before had been done either by phone, email or in satellite offices in the Pentagon. Finally seeing this place for real, he felt like he'd died and gone to some weird heaven.

It was Sunday and two in the afternoon when he and Maura arrived. The place looked dead; the parking lots were mostly empty. After passing through a lengthy security process at the main entrance, they started walking the building's long hallways, trying to figure out where to go. There were no signs, no directions on how to get anywhere. It was only that they found a woman in a copying room who turned them in the right direction that they were finally on their way.

They were both dragging by now. After flying five hours—commercial, in separate seats—they'd Uber-ed here direct from the airport, jet lagged and surviving only on lots of caffeine. Despite this, Starr had been quieter than usual since landing. Maura finally mentioned it as they neared their destination.

"Is it something I said?" she asked. "Or have I just been blabbing too much?"

He shook his head twice.

"No and no," he told her. "It's just that I'll be meeting my new boss for the first time today and I'm sure they went to town on my background check, and you never know what they're going to find in those things."

Translation: *Now* was the time he had to worry about Angel, him and their unauthorized use of the Tomato Cans.

His old boss, Admiral Thomas Hawley, had resigned in disgust after their last mission together, which spookily uncovered an unauthorized dark op aimed at hacking into American network TV and distorting its content.

Starr knew nothing about his new commander, not even a name. Security was ultra-tight at the ONI, and because NILE was one of its murkier units, names only came up during a first meeting.

But if the new boss was anything like his old bosses, they'd be tough, smart and by design, a Grade-A prick.

This was why he was anxious.

They reached Room 1391, third concourse north.
This was the place.

There was a triple-lock security system on the outside door. Starr fed it two IDF cards and then had his retinas scanned. A light on the door flashed green.

There was a small waiting area nearby. Maura would stay here during his debrief, on hand in case the Brass wanted to ask her anything before she flew back to the Emerald Isle. Starr left his gig bag with her.

He went through the door to find a small vestibule with a glassed-in office at one end; it had smoked windows so it was nearly impossible to see inside.

No one was manning the outer area so he cautiously walked into the darkened office. Behind the desk sat the woman they'd met earlier in the copying room, the one who had directed them here.

She looked different. She'd put on her uniform jacket and changed her hair. Suddenly someone he thought was someone's administrative assistant turned out to be his new boss. Angel would have scolded him for assuming she was just a secretary and she would have been right.

But while he was sure that she was tough and smart, the new boss was, as the kids say, smoking hot.

He delivered his best possible salute, at the same time apologizing, for what he did not know.

She enjoyed his discomfit, waiting a few moments before finally standing, returning his salute and offering her hand.

"Admiral Joan Millflower. New director of NILE. You must be Lieutenant Starr, our ESP expert . . ."

"Yes, I am . . . ma'am . . ."

Starr had an unusual type of ESP called short-term partially advanced precognitive ability. He usually saw things not in the far future, but just a second or two before they happened. In the Navy shrinks' vernacular, this was called "pre-cog shrinkage." And it was because of this odd ability that he was part of NILE, though he didn't see ESP coming into play very much in this new, strange case.

She indicated he should sit. She was probably 45, blond-ish, movie-star looks and shape. No wedding ring.

"I read your preliminary text," she began, leaning forward on her desk. "It was enough to get me here on a Sunday. So please, fill me in on the rest . . ."

Starr launched into his report. No visuals; it was all verbal and he told her everything: Catching the Friendly case, hooking up with Maura, chasing the priest through Ireland and wondering the whole time how he'd been able to win the ten million dollars in the first place.

He told her the idea the priest had been cheating somehow had crossed their minds—what else could it be? But what Maura and her brother found had changed all that. Maybe there *had* been another reason. Maybe he'd hacked into a god-like satellite up there somewhere.

His new boss listened intently, raising her eyebrows at all the right places. But by the end of it she seemed as baffled as he.

He gave her a copy of Finny's thumb drive containing all the encrypted documents they'd received from Dublin. Then, with no way to avoid it, he showed her the little coffin-shaped box with the Tomato Can inside, and detailed the sat-phone's connection to the mystery.

"Oh my God," she exclaimed on seeing it. "This is a museum piece. I didn't think anyone in ONI even used them anymore."

Starr remained tight-lipped, fighting off the saying-too-much syndrome.

She picked up the Tomato Can and activated it. Starr's 'Can was in his gig bag which he'd wisely left with Maura. His nightmare would have been the Admiral dialing a number and the thing ringing in his pocket in response.

But that didn't happen.

She turned it off, gathered it up with the little coffin and the thumb drive and asked Starr to wait.

Then she disappeared through a non-descript door at the other end of the smoked-in office and he was suddenly alone.

Many thoughts went through his head. To get busted for unauthorized use of the Tomato Cans would definitely be career-ending and possibly even bring time in the brig. But he didn't regret it—not really. During some of the darkest moments in some of his hairiest missions, he'd been able to hit a button and talk to the most comforting voice in the world.

Angel's . . .

So at least he'd be doing time in the clink for love.

The Admiral was gone 20 minutes—an eternity for him.

Starr was not a fan of enclosed spaces. He just wanted her to return, tell him job well-done and that he should never speak of it again and that ONI would impress the Irish National Police to impress the same on Maura. Another long cross country flight would await him. He'd be home around 2 A.M.

But then she reappeared with only the Tomato Can in hand.

She sat back down at her desk, made a quick phone call to someone—and seconds later, Maura walked in. Unexpected to say the least.

The Admiral explained: "You will both want to hear what I have to say now." At that moment, Starr was convinced he'd been caught.

But she, too, was full of surprises.

She took a moment and then said: "A preliminary review shows that no U.S. intelligence agency operates or even knows of any satellite such as this. And neither do our adversaries."

Starr was surprised. He'd just assumed that Maura's super-satellite belonged to somebody real deep in the U.S. intelligence community and that Father Friendly had somehow hacked into it via an old Tomato Can.

He politely asked the Admiral to repeat what she'd said, just to make sure.

She did so with a shrug. "We don't know of anyone's satellite technology that can do the things you've described."

When Maura began to differ, the Admiral simply held up her hand, and quickly added: "But I'm not saying it doesn't exist. The documents on that thumb drive certainly point to something afoot; I'm not sure what. When we are through here, I plan to call my friends at the Pentagon to see if it's even possible to hide something in orbit these days. But . . . if this thing really is up there and we don't know about it, then we have a major problem on our hands."

Another breath; she looked up at Starr. "So, here's your new assignment. We want you to find out how Father Friendly did it and what led him to do it. If you can do that, while we're back here behind the scenes, looking for this damn thing, maybe we'll all get lucky at the same time."

In other words, she wanted him to re-trace what Father Friendly was doing in the days leading up to his visit to the Boston casino.

And . . . she wanted Maura to go with him.

"You two are already all over this," the Admiral said. "No sense in breaking that up now."

Saying she'd already cleared it with the Irish National Police, the Admiral bestowed a very high, if temporary, security clearance on Maura, something that mildly shocked both her and Starr.

But the real shock was yet to come.

"I expect this mission is going to be travel-heavy," the Admiral continued, passing them Father Friendly's complete service file. "So you will have the use of a . . ." she checked her notes. ". . . a Gulfstream GX-79. Do you know it, Mister Starr?"

He did. The Gulfstream GX-79 was a classified aircraft, basically a very expensive supersonic business jet re-designed for special ops. But he could barely nod as a reply. He sometimes had trouble getting the Navy to reimburse his mileage while using his own car on the job. Extravagance was never part of their brief.

"A Gulfstream, but no crew," she went on. "We have to keep the footprint on this very low . . ."

"Just us two?" Starr suddenly blurted out.

The Admiral smiled and nodded.

"Yes, just you two," she said, adding. "You do know how to fly, don't you, lieutenant?"

Chapter Three

Before he became one of the Navy's X-Files guys, Starr had trained as a naval aviator.

He'd completed his primary flight qualifications and had trapped and launched off an aircraft carrier twice before his psychic abilities were uncovered by Navy shrinks and he was transferred to NILE.

So, yes, he knew how to fly—but a supersonic Gulfstream? That would be like the owner of a Chevy Impala climbing into a Lamborghini.

But those were the orders.

They picked up the GX-79 at Joint Base Andrews, Starr taking a half hour to go over the controls before they were ready to go.

But to where?

While he was reviewing his new toy, Maura had gone through her brother's Father Friendly documents and, combined with information in the priest's service file, put together a rough timeline of his activities a couple months before that fateful night at the Encore Boston casino.

Though it had a few holes in it, the timeline revealed that leading up to his disappearance, Friendly had been in both Iraq and Syria on classified missions, odd for a chaplain. Then, after recovering at the giant U.S. military hospital in Ramstein, Germany, from injuries suffered during one of those missions, he'd accepted an assignment to the U.S. Navy Sixth Fleet headquarters, which was located in Naples, Italy. But he never reported for duty. Not two weeks later, he was dead.

So, Naples seemed as good a place as any to start.

Now all they had to do was get there.

***

Take-off went well.

The GX-79 was highly automated; once at altitude, Starr punched in their destination and turned it over to the autopilot. The plane featured extra-large gas tanks, so this would be a one-hop flight. From Maryland to Naples—4,500 miles, 850 knots on super-cruise, equaled about a five-hour flight.

Starr and Maura were comfortable with each by now. They'd spent an intense two-day, hundreds of miles long chase of Father Friendly through the Irish Republic together, so they'd done this type of thing before. As everything was on automatic, and as she'd had no real rest for a while, he suggested she retire back to the luxurious passenger cabin and get some sleep.

But that was not her.

As long as he was strapped into the pilot's left hand seat, watching over everything, she would stay beside him, in the right hand seat, sharing the burden, whatever the burden might be.

Plus, she liked to talk.

And he liked listening to her.

Doing so was an exercise in stream of consciousness, though—with a distinctly Irish twist. Her family, school, jobs, family, the Catholic Church, music, myths and family once again. One thing somehow always leading to the next.

But about halfway across the Atlantic, she suddenly stopped talking. In the darkened cockpit, she had fallen asleep mid-sentence and had slowly slipped down in her seat until her head was resting on Starr's right shoulder.

He didn't dare move because he didn't want to wake her.

So that's how they stayed the rest of the way to Italy.

The Admiral had also granted them carte blanche for the mission, only because they were less likely to be made as undercover agents if they were staying in luxury somewhere.

Not wanting to disappoint his new boss, Starr had booked them into adjoining suites at the *Palazzo Carac-*

ciolo, Naples' most exclusive hotel. Right on the water, $1,200 a night, U.S.

They arrived at Naples International Airport, stuck the GX-79 in a private hangar and taxied to the hotel. Only after scanning both rooms for electronic bugs did they retire to their separate quarters and he finally got to sleep—for about three hours.

A text from Maura woke him up. It read: Gone shopping.

That was another perk of this odd mission. Before they departed ONI, the Admiral, realizing that Maura had very little in change of clothes, told her she could buy anything she wanted where ever they went and ONI would pay the bill. Again, this was the same organization that Starr hounded for weeks to cut him a $210 mileage check.

He fell back to sleep, but not for long.

He heard the high-pitched buzzing, and knew the sound immediately, even in slumber. It wasn't a cell phone; it was a Tomato Can. *His* Tomato Can.

He pulled it from his gig bag, adjusted its little satellite dish and then hit activate.

It was Angel.

He was upset but glad. Any personal calls were forbidden during NILE special ops. Using the Tomato Can, especially now, was also highly risky. But he just loved talking to her.

She was in Toronto doing a shoot for Ms. Magazine and was in between set-ups. She relayed the usual backstage gossip and then he briefed her as much as he could about why he was in Italy.

"And how is my new bestie, Maura?" she asked.

"Having the time of her life," Starr replied.

"Well, give her a big kiss for me," Angel told him.

***

As soon as Starr put the Tomato Can away, his cell phone began buzzing.

It was another text from Maura. She was at the pool and was ready for a morning brief. Giving up on any more sleep, he got dressed, found his shades and followed the signs to the *pozza*.

He stopped at the entrance, scanning the dozen or so discrete patrons gathered in pods all around the sunny, Olympic-sized pool.

It took two sweeps before he finally spotted her. He'd expected she'd be sitting at one of the poolside tables, in the shade, drinking tea in her new work-day wardrobe, laptop at the ready.

Instead she was practically right next to him, stretched out on a chaise lounge in an extremely revealing *Brioni Ginilli* bikini, appropriately emerald green.

Privé Revaux sunglasses in place, Bloody Mary at hand, she was more than stunning. This was a different kind of beauty. Like seeing the sexy librarian at the beach.

She enthusiastically waved him over. He took the chaise lounge next to her and sat on the end.

"Do you like my new suit?" she asked him.

"I'm guessing you can't buy that in Ireland," he replied, trying hard not to look, but failing.

She was totally without guile; that's what made her so sexy. Good thing he was wearing his shades and somewhat baggy pants.

She took a long sip of her Bloody Mary and then looked at him and smiled. "So, what do we do today?"

Chapter Four

Its official name was U.S. Naval Support Activity, Naples, but in reality, it was the headquarters for all U.S. naval forces in Europe including the mighty 6th Fleet.

Located right next to the airport, in the *Capodichino* section of the city, Starr and Maura arrived at the place at 10 A.M., their first stop of the day.

It was a gigantic complex, right on the immense Naples harbor, with lots of U.S. warships and support vessels tied up close by. From here the Navy conducted all its operations around the Mediterranean and beyond.

Starr and Maura knew from Father Friendly's service dossier that while recovering from his wounds at the hospital in Ramstein, the priest had been offered an honorable discharge with a medical certificate.

He refused. Instead he agreed to take the open job as chaplain at the Navy's 6th Fleet headquarters.

But again, he never reported for duty.

Once inside the main operations building, Starr and Maura introduced themselves to the base's executive officer, a full commander named Mike Robinson. A bulldog of a man, his walls decorated with photos of his days as a carrier pilot, he greeted them formally and indicated he had fifteen minutes tops.

When they told him they were simply gathering information for a pending posthumous Medal of Honor award for Father Friendly, Robinson didn't seem to believe them. But then again, he didn't have to.

Yet, while the Medal of Honor story was just their cover, by the end of the meeting, Starr and Maura would be convinced the priest deserved one.

Or two.

Or maybe even three.

Robinson began by telling them about a mission Friendly's SEAL team had run on the Iraqi-Turkish border about two months before he died. The six-man unit, plus Friendly, was airlifted onto a mountaintop in search of a remnant cell of Al Qaeda in Iraq. But blinded by fog and freezing rain, their helicopter landed in the wrong spot and was ambushed. All six SEALs were wounded before they made it ten feet from the aircraft.

Under heavy fire, Friendly loaded them back onto the helicopter, only to have an RPG make a direct hit on the flight deck, killing the pilots, crippling the aircraft and knocking the priest unconscious for a few moments.

Once he came to, Friendly used the copter's mini-gun to hold off the enemy until night fell. Then, under cover of darkness and the driving rain, he carried each wounded SEAL down the side of the mountain, one by one, returning each time until all were safe.

Every man survived. Friendly later led a second mission back to the mountaintop to retrieve the bodies of the two copter pilots.

Friendly's commanders actually *did* put him in for a Medal of Honor, but Washington was reluctant to give such an award to a chaplain who really wasn't supposed to be fighting. Add that the mission itself was highly classified and the request was turned down.

Whether this affected Friendly in any way or whether he even knew about the snub, it didn't deter him the next time he faced hostile fire.

That happened a month later in the northeast corner of Syria. Targeting a known hideout of some ISIS diehards, Friendly went in with a snatch team, hoping to capture the group's leader and put the rest of his gang out of action.

But again things went wrong right away when the two copters landed in a minefield. Both hit mines, both were disabled.

Once again, Friendly was the only person not injured in the landing. He immediately called for help, thinking the copters had been hit by ground fire. Once he realized they'd come down in a minefield, he frantically called back to the rescue helicopters and told them no matter what happened, they could not land for fear of setting off more mines.

Instead, he had them come in just a few feet above the ground and hover so he could lift the wounded soldiers aboard for evacuation. He did this under enemy fire for more than thirty minutes. Finally he climbed aboard the last rescue copter himself and was carried out of the area.

Once again, every man survived. Once again, Friendly was put in for the Medal of Honor.

Once again, the Brass deep-sixed it.

As astonishing as these two missions were, they almost paled to what Friendly did just three weeks before his disappearance. It became known as the Evacuation of Kur Peak.

It was another mountain top; another armed insertion by helicopter. This time the operation was not classified, though. It was a rescue mission and everyone involved was a volunteer.

Located in far northeastern Afghanistan, close to the Chinese border, the area around Kur Peak had recently come under control of a religious warlord who had a reputation for abusing children.

There was a Christian mission exactly halfway up the mountain that served as a home for orphans of war victims. Facing unspeakable horror at the hands of the warlord and his soldiers, the CIA asked Friendly's SEAL team to go in and rescue the kids.

There were 22 orphans at the mission, plus seven adult staff. This was too many for a safe night time recovery, so a plan was hatched. The SEAL team would land at the top of the mountain and descend from the peak. Meanwhile, a troop truck owned by a local allied militia would drive up to the orphanage, link up with the SEALs, load everyone on-board and then drive back down.

But as these things sometimes go, the evacuation was a clusterfuck from the start.

Because of the urgency of the situation, the SEALs had to rely on the Pakistani air force to chopper them in. That was mistake number one. The landing area was enveloped in a snow squall when they arrived. Just before touching down, the pilots lost their nerve and aborted the landing—but only after Father Friendly had already jumped out.

Left alone but undeterred, the priest made his way through the blinding snow, down the mountain, finally reaching the orphanage.

Here he found even more disorder. The militia truck had arrived, but the driver had fled after spotting a band of the warlord's fighters, torches in hand, coming up a path on the opposite side of the mountain.

With the bad guys just minutes away, Friendly quickly loaded the orphans and staff onto the truck, broke out its windshield and affixed his M-2 rifle to the dashboard. The weapon was equipped with a K2 grenade launcher of which Friendly had eight rounds. He also had three clips of ammo for the rifle.

Climbing behind the wheel, he drove the truck down the mountain, firing the grenade launcher and his rifle at everything and nothing. The result sounded like a column of tanks shooting their guns and descending the peak at high speed. The racket spooked the warlord's fighters long enough for the truck to get away.

Friendly eventually hooked up with another SEAL unit. All the kids were safe as were the staff members. But only then was it discovered that somewhere along the way, Friendly had suffered a serious, but almost invisible wound to his skull. He couldn't remember how and when it happened, but it possibly occurred when he was knocked unconscious during the first of the three missions.

He was evacuated to an Army aid station and then on to Kuwait, then flown to Ramstein. According to his dossier, he was treated for a hairline skull fracture and a severe concussion.

It was then Robinson mentioned, almost in passing, that during his recovery, Friendly told doctors he was having recurring dreams about being a reincarnated member of the Knights Templar.

Robinson sent them on to the 6th Fleet's chief intelligence officer. He was Captain Gary Olsen, a sunny Virginian who, it turned out, was a protégé of Admiral Millflower when they served together at the Pentagon a few years before.

Sitting in his spare office on the top floor of the headquarters' main building, Starr rattled off their cover story to him, which had gained a certain degree of plausibility by now. They were just following up on the priest's activities prior to his death, to see if there was anything that might taint his being awarded the Medal of Honor—or three of them—posthumously.

Again whether Olsen bought it or not didn't matter. He seemed happy to share what he knew about the mysterious Navy chaplain.

"He landed safely at Naples Airport because he shows up on their security tapes," Olsen told them, reading from notes on his laptop. "And it's not unheard of for a transferee to get a little bit more R&R in before reporting to duty. They meet someone along the way or they lose track of time and we find them in a bar or a brothel.

"But that would be odd behavior for someone who was both a priest and a SEAL. Plus he was privy to classified information and participated in many black ops. His falling into the wrong hands could be problematic.

"So, by procedure, we contacted the Italian National Police first with a request they look for him. They had some sightings but nothing panned out. After twenty-four hours, we called in the NCIS guys."

The NCIS, Naval Criminal Investigation Service, was the U.S. Navy's cadre of civilian detectives, in many ways its investigative police force. One team was assigned to the Naples base.

"NCIS has technology the Italians do not have," Olsen went on. "They can get their fingers in a lot of places and by using surveillance algorithms, they'd be able to pick up Friendly's movements via his cell phone, texts, credit-card purchases, debit cards, Ubers, no matter where he was in the country. His electronic trail, shall we say. Well, it turns out, his fingerprints were everywhere in Naples—but, interestingly enough, mostly in dive bars and what, the Italians call 'club *prive*'—as in private clubs."

"And they are?" Starr asked.

Olsen shrugged and replied: "Back in the States, they're known as swing clubs—and I don't mean swing dancing. I mean husbands and wives having extra-curricular activities with other husbands and wives. Again, very peculiar for a man who's taken a vow of chastity."

Starr shot a glance at Maura who was wearing the strangest smile. "Maybe he was trying to save some souls," she said.

"Maybe," Olsen went on, not missing a beat. "But whatever he was doing, NCIS got close to him a few times, only to lose him at the last minute. Still it was enough to convince them that our priest went missing on purpose, so it went from a possible abduction case to one of AWOL."

"And that was it?" Starr asked.

"Pretty much," Olsen replied. "His trail eventually went cold and, as you know, he died a couple weeks later. So they closed the case."

But the abrupt end didn't sit well with Starr.

"What was the closest they got to him while the case was still open?" he asked Olsen.

The intelligence officer checked his notes again. "They thought the algorithm picked him up on a security camera in a bar they were monitoring, but he went out the back door before they could get anyone there. In fact, that was the last time he was seen, at least in this country. He disappeared for good right after that."

"Do you have the address in Naples where that happened?" Maura asked.

More note checking, then Olsen replied: "Actually it didn't happen in Naples. It happened down in Rome, at some dive bar called Salotto 42."

He showed them the security camera's video clip on his laptop. It was barely ten seconds long. The person of interest leaves a table in the background, walks to the bar and displays a handful of bills. The money is collected by someone off camera with tattoos on their arms. Then the subject looks directly into the camera before snuffing out a cigarette and leaving by the kitchen door.

The video was fuzzy and in grainy black and white, but to Starr and Maura, the person in it sure looked like the wayward priest.

"Did anyone ever follow up on this?" Starr asked.

Olsen shook his head.

"Not that I can see," he replied. "It says here the NCIS guys eventually decided it was a false lead."

"Why?" Maura asked.

Olsen shrugged again. "Because Rome is three hours away and Friendly's electronic trail never left Naples that day. I guess they figured he couldn't be in two places at once."

***

They left the 6th Fleet base soon after, Starr driving their high-end Audi Cabriolet rental car.

Regrouping at a street-side café Maura had spotted while shopping near the hotel, they ordered cappuccinos and heavily iced cake and discussed what they'd found out—and what they hadn't.

"Believe me," Starr said. "Friendly would know how to go to Rome and make it seem like his electronic trail was still here. He's a SEAL. He's an expert in adapting and deception. Getting somewhere three hours away while staying off the radar would be no big deal for him. He might have just jumped on a bus, paid in cash and left his cell phone behind. Or maybe he hitchhiked."

"Shouldn't Captain Olsen have known that?" Maura asked. "I mean, he knew enough about the places Friend-ly was frequenting."

Starr shrugged. "Maybe. But the real question is, why did Friendly go to Rome first—no luggage, no credit cards, no phone—and *then* disappear?"

They both thought for a few moments, in between bites of iced cake.

"He got conked on the head pretty good during one of those three missions," Maura finally said. "Maybe he was winking out. I mean, the Knights Templar angle is pretty wild. Could be he lost a screw or two."

Starr sipped his *cappa.* "But he was on the ball enough to somehow tap into a super-duper secret satellite a week later," he replied. "And then use it to win ten million dollars. If he lost a screw, it sounds like one he didn't need."

She couldn't disagree, scraping the last of the frosting from her plate. "So, now what?"

Starr looked at the bill.

"Ever been to Rome?" he asked.

But Maura wasn't listening. Three young men had passed by their table, one uttering a sexist profanity in her direction.

Without a word, she got up and followed them out of the place. By the time Starr left some money and caught up with her, she had the offender pressed up against a wall and in loud English was telling him he wasn't man enough to do what he'd so vilely suggested.

The man was terrified—his friends were puzzled. Starr arrived, diplomatically freed the perpetrator and with one look, suggested he and his buds resume walking.

Maura yelled at them as they retreated, questioning the sexual capability of all three.

It was no excuse, but Maura was dressed in fine Italian summer clothes—she looked gorgeous. Still Starr was surprised by her actions, not that she had launched a verbal counter-assault but that on the sly, he saw at the same time she had the guy backed against the wall, she'd shown him—and only him—that the tip of her Glock service revolver was pointed right at his manhood.

That's how Maura handled the situation. She *never* ceased to amaze him.

But it all went away just a few seconds later, when Starr's short-term sensory ability suddenly clicked on. He turned to see a delivery van parked nearby—with the man in the passenger seat, taking their picture. Maura saw him too. Once spotted, the van took off and disappeared down the street.

It was all over in just a few seconds, but she was as surprised as he.

"Who the hell would be following us?" she wondered.

Chapter Five

They were on their way to Rome thirty minutes later.

Starr was at the wheel, top down, Maura's dark red hair and silk Italian scarf flowing in the wind.

She *loved* to talk. Starr loved listening to her and her Irish lilt made everything sound sweet and sexy at the same time.

They began the three-hour drive south with theories of who would be watching them, taking pictures of them, maybe tailing them.

But there were few suspects. The only people who knew they were in Naples worked for the U.S. Navy. And as far as they were concerned, their mission was just a glorified security check to make sure Friendly was clean enough to get the Medal of Honor, despite the screwiness in the last few weeks of his life.

True, they'd almost been killed in Ireland a few months before while tracking the priest; Albanian assassins, paid by the Russians to eliminate Father Friendly, wanted Starr and Maura out of the way too. But they escaped and their would-be killers wound up dead themselves, dispatched by none other than . . . Father Friendly.

So, it wasn't them.

Past enemies of Starr? He was sure none of them knew he was here. Friends of the Irish gangsters they busted at the climax of the Friendly chase? Italy was a long way to go to seek revenge, especially when there were so many other people still in the British Isles they could harm.

Ghosts of Maura's past arrests?

"Most of them couldn't find Italy on a map," she said.

Maybe it was just a fluke, a local taking pictures of a beautiful girl up in the face of a Neapolitan would-be lothario.

But they both knew, from their combined years of investigative experience, that in undercover work, flukes were extremely rare.

The place where NCIS thought they'd caught Friendly looking into a security camera was no dive bar.

Just the opposite. Close by the Via del Corso, Salotto 42 might have been the chicest *barretta* in Rome, or at least one of them. Laying claim to making the best drinks in the world, it also had killer views of the Vatican nearby.

Starr and Maura walked in, playing the part of a couple. The place was near-empty with plenty of tables available. But they took seats at the very end of the bar, next to the kitchen door and right under the same security camera that had caught Father Friendly—or someone who looked like him—staring into it. An ashtray indicated this was the only place in the restaurant where patrons were allowed to smoke.

The video clip Olsen had shown them had been time-stamped around one in the afternoon; it was just about that now. But it seemed like an odd time to be in a place obviously designed for the nightlife.

"Maybe he was meeting someone here," Maura said, scanning the place. "And he knew there wouldn't be a lot of people around. You'd leave around one if you've just finished lunch."

"Unless you're Italian," Starr replied. "Most Italians don't eat lunch until one and can still be eating at 2:30 or even 3 . . ."

"Why the hit and run then?" she wondered.

They both ordered a whiskey and water from a table waitress doing double duty behind the bar. She delivered their drinks and then disappeared.

"Maybe . . . he was meeting an American," Starr said, clinking his glass with hers. "Someone who *would* eat lunch at noon."

He recounted what they'd seen on the security tape. Friendly appears to throw a bunch of cash at an unseen, tatted-up employee, looks directly into the camera and then leaves.

"But who goes out by the kitchen door?" she asked. "It's an odd thing to do."

"It's a good way to get your ass kicked in some places," Starr noted. "Not many chefs are touchy-feely and they usually guard their territory like hawks. So why's this guy okay to leave by the back door?"

She thought a moment. "He knew someone here," she said. "Or that transfer of cash was his way of making a new friend."

Starr checked his watch. "We might have to sit here all day to find out," he said,

"Duty calls," she replied, this time tapping her glass against his.

He didn't need whiskey to once again appreciate how unusually attractive she was—but it sure helped. On top of that giant smile, there was a very mysterious beauty about her. He wouldn't have minded at all spending the whole afternoon here with her.

But it was not to be.

The waitress who'd served them had been replaced by a male bartender. No more than 30 years old and appropriately swarthy, his arms were severely tatted from the wrists up.

"Where have we seen him before?" Starr asked under his breath.

"Do you have any American cash?" she replied. Starr pulled out his greenback reserve—ten ten-dollar bills. She snatched two of them and said: "Leave this to me . . ."

As he could sometimes do, Starr thought he saw the next few seconds before they happened. Maura catches the bartender's eye, not hard to do, he walks over, she discretely shows him the cash and sweet talks him into making a deal.

But his short-term ESP wasn't always right.

Instead Maura loudly called the bartender over, threw the twenty dollars onto the bar and then stuck a picture of Father Friendly in his face.

"Do you know this man?" she asked, like a big sister talking down to a cranky little brother.

But still, Tats fell under her spell.

"Maybe, maybe," he stuttered in a heavy accent. "Why do you ask this?"

"He stole some jewelry from me," she replied, matter-of-factly. "My attorney and I would like to get it back. How do you know him?"

The bartender continued to wilt; he couldn't take his eyes off her.

"The same way I know you," he replied, still shaky. "He showed me cash one day . . ."

"And he paid you to go out the back door?"

Tats nodded. "He'd finished lunch and that's the way he wanted to leave."

"Why?"

Tats shrugged. "No idea . . ."

"Was that the only time you saw him?"

More nodding.

"Who did he have lunch with?"

The bartender thought a moment.

"A woman," he finally replied. "Attractive, but older than you. He seemed taken with her."

"What else was unusual about him?" she asked. "Besides paying you to go out the back door?"

The man bit his lip, indicating he was thinking deeply. Then the light went on.

"I heard him repeat the same phrase with her many times," he said. "He was trying to memorize it and the woman was talking him through it, coaching him. Their voices were hushed . . ."

"How did you know what they were saying then?" Starr interrupted.

Tats just shrugged again and replied: "In this place, I hear everything . . ."

Maura gave Starr a look, as if to say, I've got this.

She turned back to the bartender and said: "Ignore him and just tell me what they were saying . . ."

Tats moved in a little closer to her. "It was something that was so very simple, I don't understand why he wasn't getting it. Or why he didn't just write it down or something . . ."

Maura shot Starr another knowing glance. Deep-cover operatives rarely wrote anything down, electronically or otherwise. It was a canon of the craft.

"So? What was he trying to remember?"

"Something in Italian," the bartender said. " '*Da papa, a fratello, a sorella . . .*' "

Both Maura and Starr thought for a moment. Neither spoke the language. Finally, Starr had to ask: "What does that mean?"

The bartender started to reply, but then stopped. He looked at Maura sideways for a moment.

"Are you a cop?" he suddenly asked her.

"Do I look like one?" she asked right back. But the light had already gone out. He pushed the twenty dollars back in her direction and said: "I don't talk to cops. In this place, for that, I will get fired . . ."

Then he walked away.

Starr went back to sipping his drink. "At least he didn't take the money," he said. "But you must know by now I don't speak Italian."

"Neither do I," she replied. "But maybe we don't have to . . ."

She reached inside her gig bag, which was just loaded with all kinds of exotic spy stuff. Taking out an ancient smart phone, she clicked on an app and then held it close to her lips.

She whispered: "In Italian, 'Da papa, a fratello, a sorella . . .' "

She waited a few seconds, then a tinny electronic voice came on and replied: "Da papa, a fratello, a sorella . . . means 'from father . . . to brother . . . to sister . . .' "

Chapter Six

It was officially known as an MSE—for Modular Security Enclosure.

But the device had a number of nicknames, including the Hut, the Tube and the Phone Booth.

It was an egg-shaped, one-person capsule that held within a telephone that could not be hacked. It was the most secure means of communication in the 21st Century.

There was one in the White House; another traveled with the President at all times. They could be found all over the Pentagon and other high security areas where conversations had to be absolutely secret.

There was also one aboard the GX-79.

And Starr and Maura had to use it to report to Admiral Millflower what they had and hadn't found.

They drove back from Rome, checked out of the hotel and returned to Naples Airport, where the GX-79 was now parked on an isolated part of the tarmac.

The high-security MSE phone was at the back of the plane, near the tiny galley. And it did look like a futuristic phone booth—if people from the future turn out to be elves.

It was now almost noon in DC, a good time to call. Starr climbed inside the booth, activated the phone and was soon talking to the Admiral's aide.

"The Admiral will join you in a few seconds," the aide told him. "And she requests both you and Detective McCann be on the call."

This presented a problem. The Tube was just that, very slender, very confining. Starr liked to think he was six foot tall. He wasn't, but still, it was a tight squeeze just for him.

If they both had to be on the call, it would be a close-quarters situation.

Very close.

A few moments of awkward twists and turns resulted, but they soon discovered the only way they could both fit and still close the door was for Maura to sit on his lap.

Starr fought mightily to stay focused, but it was tough. She smelled great, felt great and she did her best to squish in as close as she could, doing so easily and without a second thought.

Starr took a deep breath and begged the cosmos to keep him centered and on task.

The Admiral came on and Starr managed to give their full report. The Naples people could have moved quicker once Friendly went missing, he told her, and maybe someone in Rome could have been contacted and brought in on the case. But in the end it didn't really matter. They were both convinced that it was the wayward chaplain on the bar's security camera and that he chose to disappear for those couple weeks before his death.

"The only real piece of evidence we have from Rome is part of a conversation overheard in the bar before he went out the back," Starr told her. "He was heard saying the same phrase over and over . . ."

"And what was it?" The Admiral asked.

Starr nudged Maura who spoke for the first time. "He was heard repeating this Italian phrase: 'da papa, a fratello, a sorella' " she said. " 'From father to brother to sister.' The witness said it was as if he was being instructed to memorize it."

"Other than some kind of talk about a family, we can't figure out what it means," Starr added.

"It's family talk all right," the Admiral told them. "As in Crime Family. A code of some kind."

Starr was jarred to hear this. Crime Family? The Mafia was connected to this?

"Do we really think Friendly was mixed up with the Mob?" he asked Millflower.

She actually laughed a little.

"Well," she said. "You *are* in Italy . . ."

The Admiral thanked them for the update and left with little more than you're doing a good job and carry on. But carry on to where?

Despite their legwork, they'd yet to come up with anything substantial on Father Friendly's activities in the days leading up to his visit to the casino, never mind how he was able to get a Tomato Can and use it on the God Satellite.

"And now she wants us to look into a Mafioso connection?" Maura asked after the phone call had ended but while still on his lap.

"Look into crime families in Italy?" Starr said as they finally climbed out of the Tube. "It would be easier to count all the meatballs in this country."

"That could be viewed as an offensive remark," she told him.

"I know," Starr admitted, adding: "Even worse, all I want now is some spaghetti and meatballs."

They found some MREs in the galley's storage compartment.

The unusualness of this mission was really starting to hit home for him. They were literally chasing down Father Friendly's ghost, someone who in life was extremely clever and resourceful, if, perhaps, a little kinky.

And they were doing so in such secrecy only they and the Admiral really knew what was going on.

But that meant they were really out here on their own—never a pleasant situation for undercover operations. One needed that link back to reality, back to leadership to give guidance when necessary and air cover if anything went wrong.

But for this one, it was just he and Maura, the supersonic business jet and a dead man whose trail went purposely cold, just when it seemed like they were just a few ticks away from solving the mystery.

Starr got his spaghetti and meatballs—it was just in the form of a freeze dried MRE whose expiration date could be measured in decades. They sat on the couches just outside the galley section and had their meal.

"OK, so let's review," Maura said, eating some faux-Chinese chop suey. "Father Friendly gets hurt in the head, recovers, leaves the hospital in Germany, flies to Naples on Uncle Sam's dime, goes AWOL, mysteriously turns up in Rome, has a mysterious lunch with who we think was a middle-aged American woman, and then paid the bartender to let him leave by the back door."

Starr sipped from his mix of a Tang-like powder and warm galley water.

"And he went out the back because, A: he thought the cops were coming?" he asked. "Or B: he *wanted* to be seen and looking directly into the camera was his way of saying: See you later, suckers."

"I can't think of a third good reason," she said. "Unless . . ."

"Unless?"

She pushed her hair back onto her shoulders.

"Unless we are overthinking this, and the good priest was simply having an affair," she replied. "Those were the kind of places he was visiting in Naples. Maybe the mystery lady's husband was in Rome or out front or something and our holy man needed a secure means of escape. Literally going out the backdoor."

Starr had to think a moment about this one.

"Do priests even have affairs?" he finally asked her.

She looked down at her plastic pouch full of gooey noodles.

"Everyone has affairs," she replied softly.

Chapter Seven

The small restaurant was called "Casa Della Vicenda."

Literally, "Home of the Affair." It was well named.

Located on Vico Detto Emanuele a few blocks from Naples Harbor, this was where rich husbands met their mistresses and rich wives looked for boyfriends. It wasn't quite a *club prive*, but it was close.

Starr and Maura walked in separately, but made sure to sit next to each other at the bar. They shared a bottle of pricey Masseto wine with a free shot of grappa courtesy of the trattoria's owner and chef, Mama Lucia Licciardi. Only then did they order dinner. White truffles with lobster for her, Kobe steak bolognaise over golden rice pasta for him. Both meals were excellent.

They ate and talked and lingered, adulterers all around them. After a while, Lucia the owner took special notice of them. She introduced herself once the dishes were cleared away and was immediately taken by Maura's sunny disposition. This resulted in more grappa.

Then she got Starr to admit that he was no stranger to little attacks of ESP. She claimed to be part psychic herself.

At their urging, she told them how the restaurant had been in existence for nearly 50 years, and that it started with her father, then was passed down to her brother and finally to her, his only sister. Cooking wasn't just their business, she told them, it was their life.

When closing time arrived, Lucia wanted to give them one last shot of grappa.

"Only if you give us a tour of your kitchen," Maura told her.

Drinks in hand, Starr and Maura followed her through the swinging doors and into the small kitchen.

Lucia began to explain about her "secret" wood-fired stove when she felt something cold against her temple.

It was Maura's pistol.

"*Non muoverti*," Maura whispered to her. "Capeesh?"

Lucia knew not to move a muscle; besides the game was already up. The small kitchen had two freezer doors. Starr opened one and behind it was indeed a freezer. He opened the second one and found six women sitting at tables, packaging bricks of Turkish heroin.

Starr waved his pistol around while Maura called the police, waiting outside. Within a minute, the half dozen packagers were being led away and Mama Lucia was handcuffed and sitting on a bench near the bar.

The raid was the result of three days investigation by Starr and Maura using information gathered from the local police and then put through an AMERC computer at 6th Fleet Headquarters. Essentially an adapted HPE Cray supercomputer, capable of millions of calculations a second, it boiled it all down for them with technology the local cops could only dream of.

They'd inputted a fairly narrow set of parameters for the AMERC. Long-time Neapolitan crime families that police suspected were run not by a male godfather but by a female gang leader.

The AMERC gave them three pops. One involved a middle aged woman and four nieces who'd been importing sardines illegally for decades. A second involved three sisters who dealt in stolen artifacts working with a ring in Athens.

The third pop was Mama Lucia. Restaurateur to the cheating class. and a perfect fit for 'da papa, a fratello, a sorella.' "

Though they had long suspected her of illegal doings, the Naples police never had enough evidence to charge Mama Lucia with anything. Finding the second freezer changed all that. The key was when AMERC noticed the restaurant claimed two freezers on their taxes yet only took delivery on enough things to fill one.

This led to other avenues, including the restaurant enjoying an inordinate number of debit card charges from Turkish nationals always in the last week of every month. A spike in heroin arrests—and deaths—citywide usually followed roughly a week later.

It added up. Da papa, a fratello, a sorella. Long-time crime family. Turkey. Heroin, all in an atmosphere of not-so-secret infidelity.

But where did Father Friendly fit in? Of all the places he'd visited while in Naples, this place was not on the list. But that could have simply meant he hadn't spent any money here.

They showed Lucia a photo of the priest but she denied knowing him. They had her cold for a Turkish connection, but did she have any contacts elsewhere in the Middle East? Syria? Iraq? She said no. Had she been to Rome lately? She replied by saying: "I've never been to Rome."

They grilled her for more than an hour, but at the end of it, they came to believe her. She was involved with the Mob, yes, but there was not even a faint dotted-line connection to Father Friendly.

They accompanied Mama Lucia to the police station, where they were asked to wait for the district chief to arrive. He wanted his picture taken with them.

He finally showed up an hour later. Lots of photos resulted and then Starr and Maura were each presented with a gold-plated medal for their investigative work.

But five minutes later they were back outside, in their Audi rental, three days wasted with little more than a tiny medal to show for it.

Even worse, the priest's trail was now ice-cold.

They returned once again to Naples Airport and the GX-97.

Drinking instant coffee with horrible powdered creamer, they went over all their notes three times, coming to the same conclusion each time: Friendly engineered his own disappearance, went off the grid for two weeks on purpose until he showed up in Boston at the Encore Casino.

They agreed the chance he stayed very long in Rome or even in Italy after the bar camera incident seemed remote. And the Admiral's suggestion to look into Mob ties went nowhere. So, what next?

When tracking a target, if the clues dried up at one known location, it was sometimes wise to move on to another location you know the target had visited recently as well, as some missing information might be found there.

Thirty minutes later, Starr was getting the final take-off clearance from the Naples tower, Maura in the right-hand seat beside him. Climbing into the night, they quickly reached 20,000 feet and then turned northwest. Starr punched their destination into the flight computer. 53.4129 North, 8.2439 W.

Next stop: the Republic of Ireland.

Chapter Eight

White's Cross
Cork, Ireland

The name of the tavern was the Bull & Chain.

It was located on the bottom level of the Glenballey Castle just outside the village of White Cross. A sign over the front door identified it as "Eire's Most Haunted Pub."

The castle was small but the real deal; high walls, drawbridge, tower, the works. Its exterior was enveloped in ivy vines hundreds of years old.

It was here, inside the tavern, that Starr and Maura first met.

At the time everybody—NILE, British Intelligence, the Irish National Police—believed Friendly was planning to deliver his $10 million in winnings to an upstart branch of the IRA. That the eventual outcome turned out to be the exact opposite was all but lost in the bizarre episode.

Even now, Starr looked back on it as nothing like a typical NILE mission, if there was such a thing. To him, the case became a graphic novel come to life.

Maura had chosen the Bull & Chain that day because Father Friendly had been in the place just a short time before. Meeting Starr there made sense from a logistical standpoint; it was where their great chase began.

But it also laid them bare to the pair of Albanian assassins who were chasing Friendly as well and saw Starr and Maura as a threat to be eliminated.

There was only one person in the tavern that day that'd seen Father Friendly—and then later on, Maura and Starr meet inside. And so it could have only been he who tipped off the Albanian gunmen about them.

That favor had yet to be punished.

Jackie Moran had been the bartender at the Bull & Chain for twenty-four years. He'd seen his share of mean drunks, tough broads and barroom brawls. He was a big guy, though; he could take care of himself.

But he also knew how to take care of the local cops with one free lunch a month. He knew how to stave off an angry wife with a free glass of wine as hubby left by the side door. He'd also been dipping the till for most of those two dozen years. Three trips to Amsterdam and one to Las Vegas was just the beginning of that story.

It was now 2 A.M. He locked up the tavern and began his quarter mile trek home, this night, like many, a journey through thick fog.

He walked over the drawbridge, out to the road and pointed himself in the right direction.

But suddenly someone was in front of him, coming out of the mist like a banshee. Before he could react he got the butt end of a nightstick square in his throat.

He collapsed to his knees, gasping for breath.

Suddenly this girl was standing over him; she was so close he could almost see up her skirt. She had a revolver in one hand, a nightstick in the other and, strange the things you see at a time like this, incredibly bright blue eyes. He could see them even in the fog.

"Remember me?" she hissed at him.

When he didn't reply fast enough, she shoved her ID badge into his face.

It was all coming back to him now.

"I swear I didn't know you was a cop," he managed to gurgle.

She slapped him hard across the face, opening his lower lip.

"It didn't make any difference if I was a fairy princess," she spit back at him. "You still tipped those button men to our location and where they could detonate their truck bomb. That made us very upset."

"I'm sorry for that . . . My God, I didn't know . . ."

"Oh really? Are you this sorry?" she asked hitting him again in the throat with the nightstick.

"Or are you *this* sorry?" she went on, kicking him twice in the groin with her Stefano Bemer heels.

Moran crumpled to the ground for good.

In much distress he looked up at Starr, standing nearby and watching Maura in action.

"For Christ's sake, man!" he pleaded. "Are you going to let her do this to me?"

Starr could only shrug and reply: "I'm just her lawyer..."

The conversation at the side of the foggy road lasted another ten minutes. The bartender sitting up and breathing again, his hands and feet bound with plastic ties. Maura did the asking and Jackie Moran was more than happy to do the answering.

The Albanians paid him two hundred Euros to provide info for their attempted hit on them. "Cheap bastards," she said.

More important the bartender spilled to them everything about his interactions with Father Friendly that day.

"He said he was a retired priest," Moran told them now. "But I had no idea he was a SEAL. He did tell me he was just in from Boston. That he was visiting relatives over here."

"Who isn't?" Maura said dryly.

Starr finally got into the act. "Did he tell you where he stayed in Boston? Or what he was doing there?"

Moran just shrugged. "He just said something about living in a monastery where traveling priests can stay instead of going to a hotel. A place right near the harbor, he said."

Interrogation over, Maura kicked Moran in the beans one more time, freeing him from his plastic hand ties but leaving him in the gutter writhing in pain.

She brushed her hair back and then looked at Starr and smiled, as if nothing had happened.

"I've always wanted to visit Boston," she said.

Chapter Nine

They returned to the GX-79, which was parked at Cork Airport in an area reserved for government aircraft.

Starr could have used a few hours sleep, but time was now a luxury. He always carried a bottle of bennies, government-issued amphetamines that would keep him up for at least 24 hours, sometimes more.

He shared a couple with Maura and they took off just as dawn was breaking over the Irish Sea.

They flew into the night, trying to beat the sun across the puddle. The classified jet was stunningly simple to fly. The auto pilot did everything including putting the plane into supersonic flight once they reached 40,000 feet.

At that point, all they had to do was sit back and enjoy the ride. It was a crystal clear night and the ocean of stars above them was amazing to look at. Both wide awake, they saw lots of things in the sky around them—other airplanes, shooting stars, and more than a few things that couldn't be identified. Flashes of light, three or four at a time, flying in formation.

Speed not only kept you awake, it also made people talk. With Maura, it was even more so.

He heard stories from her grade school on up through the police academy. She recited some poetry. She sang a few songs a capella, betraying a beautiful voice. They played a word game. She told him about firing her first gun and then confessed she had developed a crush on Angel.

"Join the club," he told her.

Just as she was wrapping up the story about her first pet dog, they began descending through the clouds, the pre-dawn skyline of Boston slowly coming into view.

They flew over the Encore Casino, conveniently located right under their approach path. It looked like a jeweled palace along the river front, a piece of Vegas pizzazz close to Beantown.

They landed at Logan International and stashed the GX-79 in a Coast Guard auxiliary hangar on the edge of the huge, always congested airport. They secured another rental, a Ford compact, which was no match for the high end Audi they'd tooled around in back in The Boot.

They would have both loved to go to the Encore, but decided against it. They couldn't imagine anything could be found there now. Plus, there was no telling what would happen if they were caught on security cameras. If the God Satellite did exist, was it tracking them now?

Did it have the ability to track any human on Earth?

They drove through the Sumner Tunnel and were soon approaching their target: the St. Anthony Shrine on Arch Street in downtown Boston. A beautiful structure nearly lost in the skyscrapers of the city's financial district and close to the harbor, it was a place where visiting priests could stay for free.

They parked the Ford and walked into the lobby to find some seriously impressive 1930s art-deco architecture. It was obvious the place was once a hotel. Sitting behind what used to be the registration desk was a jumbo-sized Franciscan monk, in full habit, Friar Tuck haircut and all.

He greeted them calmly, not seeming surprised to see two well-dressed 20-somethings standing before him, as if they'd mistaken the place for a high-end inn.

Maura went into her cover story. In a perfect American accent, she told the monk that her uncle was an elderly priest who had not been in contact with the family lately. They knew he spent at least one night at the monastery somewhat recently. They'd lost track of him after that.

As her lawyer, Starr displayed a photograph of Father Friendly and took note of the look of recognition on the monk's face. He'd seen the priest at least once before.

"I can't be sure if he stayed here or not," the monk lied.

"How many guest rooms do you have?" Maura asked.

"Four in all . . ."

"Can we see them?" Starr asked.

The monk was growing agitated. He was no longer in his comfort zone.

"And for what reason?"

Maura replied: "That my uncle may have left something behind and . . ."

The monk held up his hand, stopping her in midsentence. "I'm afraid we have privacy issues here that would prevent that sort of thing."

Maura kept her cool and her accent. She looked around the opulent lobby and asked him: "Did you take a vow of poverty, brother?"

Starr grimaced. Uh-oh. Meow . . .

"That's also private . . ." the monk scratched back.

They returned to the car and climbed into all dark clothing—black jeans and t-shirts. Everything but the ski masks.

They went around to the back of the monastery, where they'd spied an ancient fire escape earlier. They'd both done this sort of thing before. They both understood sign language. They both had their hand weapons out.

But Maura couldn't resist telling him one more thing.

"Breaking into a monastery?" she whispered. "What would my mother think?"

Up the fire escape, through a third floor window, along the darkened hallways until they saw a sign for the visitors area.

They found four rooms—though they looked more like barracks than a hotel. Very Spartan, a bunk, a chair, a small end table and an ancient television set in each.

They'd obviously been recently cleaned; the scent of Pine-Sol was everywhere. But one room was not like the rest. One smelled just slightly of cigarette smoke—and watching the Italian bar room security tape, they knew Fred Friendly, priest and SEAL, was also a smoker.

"He couldn't resist taking a few puffs in here," Starr said.

"Like any addict, he might have hidden the tools of his trade somewhere," Maura replied.

They slipped into the room and quietly tossed the place.

It was Maura who found it. Way under the bunk, caught up in the springs was a book of matches. It was from a bar in Ghost Creek, Arizona, called Krackers. It billed itself as the most haunted saloon in the American West.

Starr couldn't believe their luck. When they were chasing Friendly through Ireland he'd stayed at several places that were billed as being haunted. And now, here it was again.

"Pure Father Friendly," Maura whispered to Starr in triumph.

But the best was still to come.

She opened up the matchbook to see something scribbled inside.

He put his penlight on it and together they read the scrawl: "*Da papa, a fratello, a sorella . . .*"

Chapter Ten

They rushed back to the airport, climbed aboard the GX-79 and squeezed back into the secure phone booth.

The Admiral took a few minutes before she came on. By that time Starr and Maura were bursting with what they had to report.

Putting together what they had found in Italy with the same mysterious phrase written on the matchbook cover, they determined that Father Friendly might have been in a desolate part of Arizona before he went to Boston, stayed over at the monastery and then went to the casino the following day.

"He must have obtained the old sat-phone somewhere along this new time line," Starr told her. "That is, after he arrived in Arizona."

"What's your analysis of that point?" the Admiral wanted to know.

"We don't have any reports of him doing miraculous things until he arrived in Boston," Starr replied. "So the first time he tapped into this super satellite must have been that night at the casino as there was nothing before. So his side trip to Arizona *must* have had something to do with the way he came in possession of the sat-phone."

"Is that your conclusion too Detective McCann?" the Admiral asked.

They were both surprised by the question.

"I concur one hundred percent," Maura replied firmly, again squirming on Starr's lap.

The Admiral put them on hold, leaving them entangled inside the tube, Maura's arms wrapped around his shoulders, his hands around her waist. The lights were very low; their lips were mere inches apart. It quickly grew into something beyond reporting to the Admiral. She looked at him—he looked at her. They'd been through a lot together. This time and before, and . . .

Suddenly the Admiral came back on the line.

"Okay, I guess you should pursue that lead," she told them. "But . . . I'm afraid that the GX-79 is needed elsewhere. You'll have to give it back . . ."

Starr didn't want to hear this. This was supposed to be a deeply secret mission. In cases like this, if the operatives can stay away from public transportation it reduced the chances their movements would be detected by any adversaries. Then the other shoe dropped.

"And we just got a memo from up top saying we have to tighten up on our temporary clearances," the Admiral said. "So I'm afraid I'm going to have to revoke Miss McCann's security pass."

Chapter Eleven

Ghost Creek, Arizona

Pastor Dave Greco was about to close up shop when there was a knock at his door.

He was proprietor of the Dreamland Chapel. It was located near the very small town of Ghost Creek, which billed itself as, among other things, the Elopement Capital of Arizona.

It was 5 P.M. His helper/professional witness had gone home long ago. The chapel organ had been shut off. The champagne chest was all locked up.

He was sure this was his helper at the door, having left something behind. But when he opened it he found a young couple standing outside. She was very pretty; he looked like a television actor.

"Sorry it's so late," she said to Greco in an Irish accent. "But we've just eloped . . ."

After losing the jet and her security clearance, Starr and Maura had been relegated to yet another road trip. This time it would be in a rental car—a Hyundai out of Boston—in which to head west, with only a balky Rand-McNally phone app to guide them.

It turned out Ghost Creek was 70 miles northeast of Tucson and near Arizona's Pinaleño Mountains. Population was less than 200. Although the app provided very little information on the tiny town, it did contain several unusual boasts: Besides being known as a great place to elope, Ghost Creek also claimed to have the best small mouth bass fishing in the southwest as well as being an ideal place to spot Bigfoot, the eponymous ghosts or even UFOs.

They'd started out from Boston with Maura behind the wheel and Starr wrestling with the map app, trying to get it to behave so he could determine the quickest way to get to Ghost Creek.

Maura was a terrible driver, though. He knew this from their previous road adventure chasing Father Friendly through Ireland. But she was also a fast driver, the faster, the better. Open highway: 75 M.P.H.? No problem. 80—90 M.P.H.? No problem. Traveling at high speed on what to her was the wrong side of the road? No problem.

In the end he just let her drive and he navigated, both while under the influence of bennies. They had to go 2,500 miles, most of it on Interstate I-44. The rental agency told them it would take 48 hours at legal speeds.

Maura made it in under thirty.

The drive gave Starr time to worry about other things too.

What happened during their last conversation with Admiral Millflower? Losing the GX-79, their home away from home, having it taken out from under them, certainly slowed down their investigation.

But Maura losing her clearance was puzzling. Why pull her credentials now, just when it appeared they were making headway on the baffling case? The timing just didn't seem right.

While he knew it would have been wise for them to put these thoughts on the back burner during the cross-country dash, the truth was they spent most of the time buzzed-out and analyzing what it all meant.

Their only conclusion was what they already knew. From Naples to Rome to Ghost Creek . . . all in less than a week. For whatever reason, Father Friendly came to the elopement capital of Arizona before embarking on his magical night at Boston's Encore Casino.

They had to find out why.

But they couldn't break cover. So on finally arriving in the tiny desert town, they knew their only option was to play the part of runaway lovers.

"Sorry," Pastor Greco told them now. "We're closed for the day."

Maura jumped right in. "You have the Enchanted Cottage, I think you call it. Is it available? We could do the ceremony tomorrow."

Greco relented. He retrieved the cottage's keys and gave them to Maura.

"How about a noon wedding?" he asked, checking his schedule. "We can discuss packages and prices then . . ."

Maura turned to Starr and said: "How's that, darling?"

"Sounds good," he managed to reply.

She shook the pastor's hand. "Thank you," she said. "Love really does conquer all, doesn't it?"

Greco smiled.

"I think so," he said.

The Enchanted Cottage was located behind the chapel. It looked like a miniature version of a typical 1950s-style house, complete with a flower garden and a white picket fence out front.

It was just one big room inside, though. Kitchen, living area, a corner for dining, all within the same space, with a mini-bathroom and shower attached. But it was the heart-shaped water bed that dominated the interior. It was gigantic and took up two thirds of the place.

A tourist guide to the area showed the bar Krackers, from where the matchbook had come, was on the other side of town, maybe a quarter mile away. It not only promised ghosts and other paranormal activity, but also the hottest chicken wings and the coldest beer in Arizona.

"I might pass on the wings," Maura told him. "But everything else sounds good."

After two quick showers and a change of clothes, they drove down the dusty main street to the north side of town. Here, they found a handful of Pueblo-style houses and a few businesses surrounded by a dozen elderly house trailers.

Krackers was clearly the center of this tiny universe. Yes, it was a bar and a sign out front boasted of its ethereal connections, as well as Bigfoot sightings and the occasional flying saucer. But the flat roof Old-West style building also housed a post office, a tire store, a feed store, a hardware store—and KRAX, the local radio station. A 50-foot white and red transmitting tower sat in the middle of its gravel parking lot.

Walking through the swinging saloon doors, Starr and Maura found the place empty. But a window at one end of the bar looked into the next room, and this was the studio for KRAX.

A man right out of a cowboy movie was at the microphone. Ten-gallon hat, handlebar mustache, leather vest, bolo tie. He saw them come in, signaled that he'd be right there and then put on Iron Butterfly's "In-A-Gadda-Da-Vida," insuring him at least 17 minutes to wait on them.

He emerged from the studio and greeted them warmly. Introducing himself as DJ Mountain Johnny, he asked when they were tying the knot.

"How did you know?" Maura replied innocently.

He displayed a tooth-gap grin and said, "Thanks to Pastor Dave and his Enchanted Shack, a lot of my clientele are lovebirds, just like you guys. I can spot you a mile away."

He set them up with two beers, but they deferred on the blazing hot chicken wings.

"How's business?" Starr asked him after a long swig. It was indeed very cold.

"Not bad considering I'm the only game in town," Johnny replied. "People always need to mail letters, feed their animals, buy some nails or fix a tire. And I'm only a ten-watt station, but we're heard all over the valley and on a good night, we can be picked up down in Tucson."

He looked around the empty saloon, and then added: "It's been dribs and drabs in here lately, though. Without Pastor Dave, I would have closed for good a long time ago."

Starr and Maura drained their beers quickly; DJ Johnny set them up again.

"What changed?" Maura asked.

He pointed to a photograph hanging behind the bar. It showed a dark mountain, mostly in shadow, covered with pine trees, with snow near the top and a blanket of fog obscuring the summit.

"That, my friends, is Mount Graham," he told them. "Ten thousand feet high, tallest of the Pinaleño mountains. Not even ten miles away."

"That explains 'Krackers' and 'KRAX," Starr observed.

"Yes—Graham Crackers!" the DJ replied. "Not everyone gets it right away."

He took down the photo so they could have a better look. On closer examination they could see a boxy structure on the mountain's peak, just barely visible through the thick mist.

"That's the Mount Graham International Observatory," the DJ explained. "One big telescope and lots of other gear. We used to have eggheads from there coming in all the time. They'd be here for lunch and back again for dinner. Not huge tippers, but they kept us running whenever the paranormal tourist stuff died down."

"But then?" Starr asked.

The DJ shrugged. "A new crowd started running the telescope," he told them. "And they're a strange bunch."

"How so?"

DJ Johnny laughed. "We are out in the middle of nowhere. If you don't drink or do something, you go nuts, right? But with these people up there now? They never party. They never make any noise. We never see them. I wouldn't know any of them if I tripped over them."

Maura showed him Father Friendly's picture. "How about this guy?" she asked. "Ever see him?"

Johnny studied the photo for a moment and then started nodding enthusiastically.

"Now, *him* I recognize," he replied. "He came in here once about two months ago and stayed almost the whole day. Nice guy, friendly. But all he wanted to talk about was Ireland and how he was planning to visit there soon."

He studied Maura for a moment. "You sound like you're from the Old Sod yourself," he said. "Is he a friend of yours?"

"In a way," she replied.

The Iron Butterfly opus was coming to an end. DJ Johnny had to change discs. But before he left, Maura asked him on last question: "Did he say why he was here?"

Johnny called over his shoulder: "Just said he had some business at the observatory."

Chapter Twelve

Starr stepped outside, asking Maura to order two more beers when DJ Johnny appeared again.

He looked to the north and for the first time took notice of the dark mountain looming over the horizon ten miles away. It looked just as it did in the photograph: Covered in pines for two thirds of the way up, then came a snow line and then the peak, shrouded in thick mist.

Can telescopes even see through fog? he wondered.

A tiny convenience store was one block away—and on spotting it Starr suddenly felt the need to take a calculated risk. Since leaving Boston, somewhere deep inside himself he'd sensed something scary and weird was looking down on him, watching his every move, hearing his every word. He couldn't help it. A nightmare of uber-technology, just knowing that something like the God Satellite might exist gave him the creeps.

But he needed some information, and getting it via his cell phone or, heaven forbid, the Tomato Can, would not be wise at the moment. At this point, he couldn't shake the notion that others would be listening in.

So he decided on a more low-tech approach.

He walked into the convenience store and spotted what he needed right away: a disposable cell phone.

Twenty dollars later, he was back out on the street. It took a few minutes to activate the burner phone, but as soon as he saw its green light blink on, he dialed a number from memory and waited.

One ring. Two. Three . . .

Then finally . . .

"Oh my God! Is this you? Are you okay?"

It was Angel—and he rarely called her cell.

"I'm all right," he told her. "Are you?"

"Yes," she replied, relief in her voice. "I'm just a little surprised that you're calling me on this phone."

"Believe me, honey. This is not the time to use the Tomato Cans. Where are you?"

"Toronto airport," she replied. "I've got a red eye to Paris for the EU Spring collection tomorrow."

He told her where he was and asked her if she could research two things for him.

"I'd love to," she said. "I've got at least another hour of waiting here."

"Question number one," he began. "Is there an ancient Roman phrase or something that translates into 'From father to brother to sister . . .?' In Italian, it sounds something like " '*Da papa, a fratello, a sorella . . .*' "

He could hear her punching the information into her smart phone.

"Got it," she told him. "And . . .?"

He looked towards the mysterious mountain again.

"Could you please get some info on the Mount Graham International Observatory in Arizona?" he said. "Like who owns it? And call me back only on this number, okay?"

They said their I-love-you and goodbyes, and then she was gone. He pocketed the phone and returned to the bar. Johnny was back and another beer was waiting for him.

"Time to go, my love," Starr said to Maura. "We've got lots to do."

He guzzled his beer as she guzzled hers. Then they paid the bill and bid DJ Johnny goodbye.

"Come in tomorrow after you're hitched," he told them. "Drinks are on me . . ."

Chapter Thirteen

The sun finally dipped below the Pinaleño mountains and dusk came to Ghost Creek and the surrounding valley.

After another clothes change, this to their all black combat utility suits, Starr and Maura drove to the foot of Mount Graham and found a fire road with a barrier blocking the way.

From here, almost two miles straight up, was the Mount Graham International Observatory, the place Father Friendly had visited just before undertaking his final mission. This was *so* odd, due diligence alone compelled Starr and Maura to investigate.

Starr made quick work of the lock holding the barrier in place, allowing their rental car to access the narrow road. Locking the gate behind them, they drove up the side of the mountain, headlights off, NightVision goggles on.

It was a slow and winding climb, snaking their way through the forest of mostly tall pines. At one point they passed a large swath of charred stumps, burned in a recent forest fire. They made for weirdly shaped shadows crisscrossing the road in front of them.

They came to another barrier about two thirds of the way up. This one was newer and sturdier and held a sign that read: No Trespassing Private Property.

The triple-lock electronic box holding it secure showed someone meant business. It was sealed tight and no matter what Starr tried, it defied his efforts to get inside and disable it.

After several minutes of frustration, he turned to Maura and asked: "When was the last time you went mountain climbing?"

***

They'd expected something like this, so they'd brought bottled water, a couple flashlights—and their weapons. A Glock for him; and this time, a Browning Hi-Power for her. Leaving the rental in a small parking area near the barrier, they started out, NightVision goggles still turned on and in place.

They were only a quarter mile from reaching the summit, but it would be an almost straight vertical climb from here. The grade was so steep Starr was amazed they'd been able to build the access road; the angle was that severe. He'd gone through high intensity training when he was with Naval Aviation, and had passed his annual fitness test for NILE every year since. So he knew he could do it.

But he just could not match Maura's enthusiasm. Once they started climbing, he could barely keep up with her.

The sun was gone by now. The stars were out, their light washing across the horizons.

The sky above them, while crystal clear, seemed almost as busy as it was over the Atlantic a few nights before. They could see dozens of blinking aircraft lights all moving in different directions, spotted at least one shooting star, and even a couple satellites. At one point, something very bright flashed over their heads, just above the treetops. It wasn't an airplane as it made no noise and they could see a distinct oval shape to it.

"That had to be a drone or something," Starr said after it had passed over.

"Or something," Maura replied worriedly.

They stayed off the road, following it up but walking in the shadows beneath the tall pines. They were trespassers at the very least and it would be good not to get caught.

But beyond the goal of reaching the top, they didn't have a plan. Once at the summit, would they just go up and knock on the observatory's front door and introduce themselves?

Maybe . . .

But they wanted to put eyes on the place first.

Thirty minutes of power climbing later, they arrived at the mountain's peak. It was very foggy at the top, the mist swirling all around them. There were a few inches of snow on the ground and the wind was blowing. They stopped at the edge of the tree line, remaining in the shadows, their NightVision goggles making everything look wavy, electric and green.

The observatory was about 200 feet away from them, almost hidden in the wind-blown vapor. It was a squared-off, window-less five-story building with an igloo-shaped dome attached. There was a parking lot out front, a loading dock out back and a windsock hanging off the roof.

That was it.

It looked pretty dull in a scientific sort of way, high above the Arizona desert, in such an isolated and lonely place.

"Why would the good father come here?" Maura wondered aloud.

Starr started to reply, but stopped. His short-term ESP began flashing.

"Someone is coming," he told her.

They stepped even deeper into the shadows and waited for about thirty seconds. Then they heard a vehicle driving up the access road, engine straining to climb the steep grade.

"That's a Range Rover," Maura whispered to him. "I can tell . . ."

She was right. A black Range Rover went by them a minute later. It went into the parking lot and stopped at the observatory's front door.

Two men got out. Thanks to their NightVision goggles, Starr and Maura could make out their faces clearly; they were mightily surprised by what they saw.

It was Pastor Greco and DJ Mountain Johnny.

"What the what?" Maura exclaimed under her breath. "What are they doing here?"

No sooner had the two men entered the building, when a brilliant orb of light came over the top of the mountain. There was no question what it was this time, though. Small, bug-like, and barely the size of a SUV, it was a diminutive Hughes OH-6 helicopter, nickname: the Killer Egg, it was a favorite of many special ops units.

Starr and Maura took yet another step back into the shadows as it came in for a noisy landing about a hundred feet away. The side door slid open and two figures climbed out. Again, Starr and Maura were startled as they recognized them as well.

"Oh my God," she breathed. "Is that . . .*Tats?*"

There was no doubt about it. It was the bartender they'd talked to at Salotto 42 in Rome just a few days before. His body ink was unmistakable.

And the man with him? The one who had actually piloted the copter? He was heavy-set but well-dressed. He also had an unusual haircut. Sugar-bowl style, except the crown of his head was shaved clean.

There was no doubt who this was either. The monk from the monastery in Boston.

Starr had been in the world of top secrets and special ops for only a few years. Still, he thought he'd seen just about everything.

But this?

"All these characters are here?" Maura whispered to him urgently. "What does it mean?"

"I have no idea," he replied in all truthfulness. "And at the moment, I wish someone would tell us . . ."

His burner phone started buzzing a second later.

It was Angel.

"You're not going to believe this," she began excitedly.

"Try me," he replied.

"Can Maura hear too? This will knock her out . . ."

Starr motioned Maura closer. She got in so tight he had to put his arm around her so they could both hear the phone.

"We're ready," she announced.

Angel took a breath and then asked: "Well . . .guess who runs the Mount Graham Observatory?"

"The Illuminati?" Starr replied as a joke.

"Almost!" Angel cried. "Turns out you could have tripped over them when you were back in Rome . . ."

Angel sometimes took the long way around when explaining things. This was one of those times.

"Once more, honey?" Starr asked.

"Okay, but let me tell you something else first," she went on. "You were led slightly astray by whoever told you the phrase, 'Da papa, a fratello, a sorella . . .'meant 'father to brother to sister.' "

"Your translator app?" Starr whispered to Maura.

She just shrugged. "Made in China . . ."

"The brother and sister part is right," Angel went on. "But the word 'Papa' could have another meaning."

"Besides 'father?' " Starr asked. "Or 'dad?' "

"Yes . . . For Italians 'Papa' can also mean Pope.' "

Starr felt his breath catch for a moment.

"Pope?" he asked.

"Yes," she answered. "In Italy, Papa—with a capital "p"—means Pope."

"*The* Pope?" he asked again, just to make sure.

"*Yes,*" Angel replied. "*The* Pope—which makes sense because—are you ready?—from what I read online, that observatory is owned by the Vatican."

Starr and Maura, still huddled together, cheek to cheek, were surprised to hear this. Both started thinking the same thing: *The Vatican runs an observatory? In Arizona?*

"What the hell for?" Starr asked Angel.

"To gaze into Heaven, I guess," she replied. "All it says is they've run it for years and tend not to make a big deal out of it."

Starr took a moment to absorb all this.

"So, the Pope has a telescope in the states," he said to Maura. "That's strange enough. But why did Father Friendly come here? And why would just about every person we met in the past week suddenly be here as well?"

They heard a noise at the back of the observatory. The rear door had opened and two figures had stepped onto the loading dock. They each threw a trash bag into the dumpster.

It was a man and a woman—but they were dressed in religious clothes. He was wearing a long brown robe with a rope for a belt and a hood to hide his face. She was in a similar habit, except she had long veils obscuring her features.

A monk and a nun.

A brother and a sister.

A fratello a sorella.

An instant later, Starr's short-term ESP kicked in again, delivering another simple message: "Look behind you."

It was like Maura heard it too, because they both turned at the same time to find six armed men in polar camo gear standing not three feet away. They'd expertly crept up on them.

"Something tells me something very weird is happening there," they heard Angel say over the burner phone.

"Something like a bad movie," Maura replied.

"I've got to go, honey," Starr told her. "Have a good flight and be careful."

"You too—I love you, Chris . . ."

"I love you, too, Angel . . ."

At the last second, Maura tipped the phone in her direction and said: "And so do I . . ."

Then Starr held up his hands. Maura did, too.

"No problems here, guys," he told the armed men. "I'm U.S. Navy. My friend here is Irish Police. Can we reach for our IDs?"

One man stepped forward and relieved them of their weapons.

"That won't be necessary," he said. "We already know who you are . . ."

Chapter Fourteen

Two guards brought Starr and Maura into the observatory while the rest of the ghostly group melted back into the woods.

Going through the front entrance, they were led down a long, dimly-lit hallway which ended with an unmarked door. One of the guards opened it, indicated they should go in and then closed it behind them.

They found themselves in a small, dark, windowless office, books and tech manuals piled up on the floor. A large screen TV hung from one wall.

There was a lone desk in the room. Sitting behind it was Starr's boss, Admiral Millflower.

His head began another slow spin as Maura grabbed his hand and squeezed it tight. Suddenly everything that'd happened to them in the past few days went upside down. Flying halfway around the world, then flying back, *then* driving two thousand plus miles, only to run into four characters from their travels, people who really shouldn't be here.

As bizarre as that was, in the sometimes crazy world of special ops, these things could probably be explained somehow.

But . . . the Admiral being here?

That was *really* strange . . .

Maura's grip on his hand tightened; Starr's mind was racing full throttle now. The Admiral's presence could only mean the Navy had been involved in this thing all along.

Which meant he and Maura had been intentionally sent on a false mission.

Which meant that the whole thing had been . . .

"A security exercise," the Admiral finished his thought for him. "Code-named 'True Blue Light.' Its purpose was to research different methods of security to protect a technology that's currently beyond our intellectual horizon. That's the official statement. And let me say, you both came through with flying colors."

She invited them to sit down. Starr collapsed into one of the two nearby chairs, his shoulders dropping like a hundred pounds had suddenly been lifted off them. His head was still spinning, but at least now, he knew they were close to getting an explanation for the fire drill of the past few days.

But Maura remained standing, still in high gear.

"Please, Admiral," she said sincerely, but sternly, "Just tell us what's going on . . ."

Millflower smiled. "Okay, I guess you both deserve a briefing on this," she said. "But be aware of two things:

First, I can't tell you everything. But second, what I *can* tell you is considered Above Top Secret, above even all Special Access levels. You'll have to sign a stack of NDAs before you leave. Plus, we'll need retina scans, photos and all cell phones sanitized. Understood?"

Starr and Maura replied in sync: "Understood . . ."

The Admiral punched three numbers into her TV remote; the screen on the wall went from black to dazzling white.

Suddenly they were looking at a roomful of consoles, monitors and communications equipment—with big screen TVs hanging everywhere. Several dozen people were hustling about, most in short-sleeve shirts and ties, doing scientific things. It looked like a mini version of NASA's Mission Control.

"All this is happening three floors below us," the Admiral explained. "It's called the Observation Level."

The camera panned around to an extra-jumbo TV monitor, hanging on the far wall of this control room. It was showing a broadcast from space. In the middle of the screen was a gigantic satellite.

It was easily the size of a city bus. Long, silver and cylindrical, two large solar panels shaped like hard-edged angels' wings sprouted from its top. It looked magnificent and mysterious at the same time. Starr wondered what skunk works it came from.

"This is OS-1," the Admiral told them. "Or what you, Detective McCann, so cleverly dubbed the God Satellite."

"So, it does exist . . ." Maura said, breathless. She finally sat down, eyes glued to the screen.

The Admiral smiled again. "It sure does," she confirmed. "And it can do everything you and your brother thought it could—and much, much more. I'm supposed to stop there, but 'artificial reality?' That was another great term by the way. This thing proves that it can be done because what you see there was created entirely via artificial intelligence. Some human gave the initial order and computers, 3-D copiers and robots did the rest. You're looking at no less than a technological miracle. We haven't even scratched the surface of what it can do yet."

Starr couldn't take his eyes off it either. The giant satellite looked like a prop from a big budget sci-fi movie.

"What is it exactly?" Maura asked.

"The grand master of all surveillance satellites," the Admiral replied. "That's the best description I ever got. A 'user-friendly flying super-computer' is another. But believe me it's so much more than that too. In addition to having the capability to see it all and know it all, you can actually talk to this damn thing and because it's filled with so much AI, it will talk back. And all you need to do is ask it for help. Like 'Tell me how to win this poker hand,' and it will process that request and come back with an answer in what has been measured in zeptoseconds—or basically no time at all.

"It was clear from its first day of inception how powerful this thing was going to be—and how dangerous too if it fell into the wrong hands. That's why Father Friendly eventually became involved. Once it was up and flying we needed someone to test its security system, to see how easy or hard it would be for someone to hack into it and use it for their own purposes. To do this required someone who'd worked special ops before, someone who was trustworthy and basically fearless. Heroic almost."

She stared at the screen for a moment, seemingly in genuine awe of the spacecraft.

"We met with Father Friendly in Italy," she went on. "And he eventually made his way here to get a good look at the OS-1. Then we gave him that outdated sat-phone and the password needed to hook up with the satellite, as if someone had stolen it. We figured a lone hacker might have less-than-ideal hacking equipment so the old sat-phone fit the bill. As for what he should do once he'd hacked in, we gave him $20,000 and asked that he attempt to increase it at least threefold.

"When he wound up winning millions of dollars, we couldn't believe how easy it was."

"So, you were the person who met him in the bar in Rome?" Starr asked her.

She nodded. "Yes, that was me . . ."

"And you knew all this when we first met you at headquarters?"

She nodded again, but with a little uncertainty. "Yes I did," she revealed. "But I had a role to play that day. At the time my biggest concern was that you, Detective McCann and her brother might not have stumbled upon this highly sensitive project out of the blue. That you might have been tipped to it.

"So we had to find out who you were exactly. And what better way than to send you on a plausible mission and have our people keep an eye on you the whole time, even though I think it's fair to say you were really bouncing all over the map for a while there."

Starr had not expected this. It almost seemed like she was saying the bizarro nature of the last few days had been their fault all along.

"But you mentioned we passed with flying colors . . ." he said.

"And you did," the Admiral replied. "Your detective work was superb. I mean, you followed the clues Father Friendly left behind, and they led you to this place. In essence, you re-traced 'the hacker's' last steps, very valuable if it ever happens for real. In our eyes that proved you're legitimate actors, because if you weren't, you certainly would not have come here. It's really the perfect ending."

"So, those people we saw arrive earlier? The bartender, the monk, Pastor Greco and the DJ?"

"All on our payroll," she confirmed. "While you were following the ghost of Father Friendly, they were following you."

"And *"Da papa, a fratello, a sorella? "* Maura asked.

The Admiral's face lit up. "That's actually legit," she said in a slightly hushed tone. "It's a nod to our landlords. It's the access code to get the satellite to pay attention to you. We gave it to Father Friendly as part of the drill, his role being that of the brilliant hacker."

"So the Vatican really does run this place?" Starr asked, still amazed.

The Admiral nodded. "Yes, they really do. And they've been nice enough to let us hide out here while we've been putting the OS-1 through its paces. It's quiet, highly confidential and can you think of a better place to hide a special ops mission than inside "a church?"

"So this is a Navy operation?" Starr asked finally.

"Let's say 'joint service,' " the Admiral said using air quotes. "We'll be here for another few months and then the Air Force will get a crack at it. After that, who knows? Whoever built this thing, the funds came out of the intelligence services budget. They're just letting us play with it for a while."

She turned off the TV.

"And for that reason," she said shuffling some papers, "Lieutenant Starr I'm immediately recommending you for a fast-track promotion to Lieutenant Commander. And I'm highly recommending to our friends in Dublin that Detective McCann and her brother are similarly recognized for their help."

She closed her laptop indicating the briefing was over.

"As I mentioned, there will be the usual security documents you must sign," she said. "And a retina scan and photos for our files, plus we have to clean sweep your cell phones.

"But besides that, I want to thank you for your participation in this. As odd as it might have seemed, you really did us, and the world, a big favor."

Chapter Fifteen

It dawned a raw and rainy morning in San Diego.

These were unusual conditions for the city that boasted the best weather in the USA, but the atmospherics seemed to match Starr's mood. Angel's as well.

They were at San Diego airport, waiting near the international gate. It would be a ten-hour flight to Dublin from here. Once up and over the North Pole, Maura would be home in time for the late Sunday Mass.

Starr was seriously bummed to see her go. They'd had spent so much time in each other's pockets over the past week and a half—and this was the second such time in less than six months. Not only did he just enjoy being around her, but this mission had ended so abruptly, though successfully, they really didn't have a lot of time to decompress. They'd driven back to San Diego, she'd stayed over at Angel's again, and they were at the airport just a few hours later.

Now, she would soon be out of his life and there was a good chance he'd never see her again.

The airport was packed and the security lines were long.

Starr and Angel waited until the last possible minute to say goodbye to Maura. Neither wanted to see her go. But the mission was over and it was now on to other things for all of them.

Angel got a long hug and a huge kiss. Starr just got the hug, but he didn't want it to end.

"Quite a week, lieutenant commander," she told him during the embrace. "Thank you for everything . . ."

"Thank you for being you," was the only thing he could say in reply.

Then she picked up her overflowing gig bag, went through security, waved one last goodbye—and was gone.

Part Two

The Skeleton Coast

Chapter One

Six weeks later

The secret airbase was 20 miles outside of Tashkent, Uzbekistan, at a place called Krasnogorsk.

Though little more than a control tower, a hanger and a fuel tank, its runway was very unusual. At 17,000 feet it was one of the longest in the world.

The Russians had built the base as an alternative landing site for its Buran space shuttle, but it was never used. The Buran program collapsed before it ever got off the ground and the airfield fell into disrepair. It still had the mammoth, three-mile long strip of cracked asphalt, though, which was good because the largest airplane in the world was about to land on it.

The first Antonov An-225 had been originally built to carry parts for the same short-lived Buran shuttle. Six engines, 32 tires in its landing gear, its wingspan was almost as long as an American football field.

That plane had been destroyed during the war in Ukraine. But thanks to donations from air enthusiasts around the world, its exact duplicate—the "B" model—had been built and then purchased by the Russian air cargo service Bystry, meaning "quickly." People familiar with the original plane say it was nearly impossible to tell them apart including its ability to carry a staggering half million pounds of cargo.

For this flight it would have to lift somewhat less than that. Still, by all accounts, it would be one of the most valuable cargo loads it ever carried.

The challenge was to do it all secretly. But could flying the world's largest airplane ever be done in secret? Someone deep in the U.S. intelligence services was going to give it the old college try.

That's why Chris Starr was here, at this long ago forgotten runway, waiting for a massive bird to drop out of the sky.

His involvement had come via a special request from the U.S. Embassy in Moscow, specifically its CIA station chief. It was Starr's first time in Uzbekistan and he felt like he was on the Moon. Desolation was everywhere he looked; it was a truly unearthly landscape. One thing he remembered from his brief was that Uzbekistan was so landlocked none of its rivers ran to the sea. It was almost claustrophobic.

He'd been here about an hour when he spotted a single navigation light coming over the mountains to the north. It took another ten minutes for the An-225B to arrive over the airfield, a modern-day pterodactyl, those half dozen engines hanging beneath its enormous wings, each spewing out a tremendous amount of smoke and exhaust.

It made a circuit of the field, then finding its nose back into the wind, began to drop . . . and drop . . . and drop. It came down so quickly, Starr was convinced something was wrong and it was going pogo into the ground.

The plane finally slammed onto the old, bumpy runway. It bounced once, but came back down and stayed together somehow. Thus began a long painful, screeching, wobbling roll-out, which at its end had the winged dinosaur using all of the three-mile long airstrip, plus the 1,000-foot dirt overshoot beyond.

This airplane cost $30,000-an–hour to lease. For that kind of money it could haul an astounding, mind-blowing 275 tons. But today, its enormous hold was carrying a human variety of cargo. His name was Dmitry Gurtovoy. Oligarch, political insurgent, and multi-multi-billionaire, his companies spent $30,000 on paperclips in the past year. Seven-foot-three and geeky rich, he was defecting to the United States—and Chris Starr would be his bodyguard for the trip.

Starr's world was a small world because he already had a dotted-line connection to the insanely wealthy Russian. Gurtovoy owned a media empire; one of his magazines was called Moscow GQZ. Angel had been on its cover three times. She'd met the mogul at several after-parties and reported he was friendly but aloof and never stayed around too long.

Gurtovoy—or "Dima" as everyone called him—lived a fairly sedate life. Despite his rumored $120 billion, he didn't own a dacha or a yacht. He split his time between apartments in St. Petersburg and Paris. He didn't swear, was a vegetarian and had championed many of Russia's environmental causes, which made him very unpopular with the regime in Moscow.

That's why he was leaving. The Kremlin had a nasty habit of sticking people they didn't like with a syringe full of poison—and Dima didn't like needles.

He wasn't a monk. He did have some hobbies. One was hanging with beautiful women, which was a breeze if you had Dima kind of money.

Another was collecting cars. Very high priced cars. In fact, he owned five of the most expensive cars in the world. And they, along with him and his entourage, were on the An-225B, on the way to his new country.

Getting Dima out of Russia itself had been the work of the CIA. Babysitting him the rest of the way was Starr's new mission.

He'd fast tracked here from San Diego, getting the gig at 8 A.M. and arriving in Tashkent 15 grueling hours later, riding in the back of an unmarked C-130 cargo plane that had no heat, no padded seats and no food. And the fun didn't end there; he'd endured a forty mile taxi ride from Tashkent to Krasnogorsk Aerodrome, all of it on roadways as bumpy as the goliath air strip.

He knew not much would change during the trip back to civilization as the An-225B was not known for its smooth ride.

But, at least it would be a direct flight.

Sort of . . .

***

The giant plane had a cover story.

It was carrying gas turbines refurbished in Uzbeki-stan for delivery to a hydroelectric power plant in South Africa. The manifest was ten pages long and full of fraudulent details.

Scheduled to land in Johannesburg around midnight, they would do the phony drop-off under the cover of darkness, then fuel-up and head northwest, towards America. Touch down at JFK was scheduled for 6 A.M. with the time change, after which Dima would be driven into Manhattan so he could buy the majority ownership in the New York Knicks pro basketball team.

His cars would fly ahead of him to their new, air-conditioned homes near Reno, Nevada. Once they arrived at this desert destination, Dima's expert auto mechanics would be the only ones allowed to even touch the precious cargo.

From there, Starr planned to rent a car and drive home to San Diego, completing his trans-global mission in just under 48 hours.

The An-225B took more than ten minutes to roll itself back to the aerodrome where Starr was waiting.

A hatch near the front wheels opened and he saw a person waving him in. Only then did Starr realize the big plane was not intending to stop. He'd have to do a sprint and jump, and hope he made it through the open doorway.

He started running and caught up to the plane, but the engine wash underneath the wing hit him like a hurricane. He was barely able to hold on to his gig bag in this mechanical whirlwind. Then, once he was close enough to the open hatch, he threw the bag inside, making enough commotion for the pilots to think he was onboard, causing them to hit the engines and suddenly double in speed.

Running full out now, Starr launched himself like Superman towards the open hatch, his fingernails barely grabbing its lip just as the pilots increased to take-off speed. Hands reached out and grabbed him, safely pulling him aboard but smacking his head on the doorway in the process.

Dazed from his entry, Starr looked up to see two beautiful women staring down at him, concern etched across their exotic features.

"If he's an American, he will live," he heard one say.

The An-225B lifted off moments later. They were airborne even before the women were able to close the hatch. Only then did Starr's ears pop and he was able to fully understand what was going on.

His first thought was one of surprise that the giant airplane had flight attendants. But the two women weren't part of the crew. They were friends of Dima Gurtovoy. Both were blonde and very attractive. Both were also wearing form-fitting flight suits with their nicknames embroidered in hearts over the left side pocket: *Misha* and *Minky*.

Had it not been for them, he probably would have missed the flight—or worse.

He got to his feet, they brushed him off and then led him up to the flight deck. His arrival there coincided with the enormous clunking sound of the plane's massive landing gear being retracted. The whole plane shook violently for several seconds while this was happening. No one except Starr seemed to notice.

In just those few moments, he learned two things about flying in an An-225B. First, old or new, it was tremendously loud, no surprise with six big engines turning and burning out on the wings. But it was also very hot inside. So hot, small personal wind fans were scattered throughout the plane, some affixed in the strangest locations. These were like air showers. The idea was to stand in front of one for a few seconds to cool off before moving back into the heat. The giant plane might have been rebuilt in the 21st century, but its technology was definitely stuck back in the 1980s.

There were a dozen extra-large fans installed on the flight deck, which was one level up from the hatchway. They too did little good as it was even hotter up here. That's why, all self-consciousness tossed aside, the five-man Russian crew was shirtless and sweaty. In that configuration, they looked more like pitmen in the Titanic's boiler room than commanders of the largest man-made design to ever fly.

The flight deck itself was huge, just like the rest of the plane. Huge and complex, with hundreds of buttons and dials and module boards and read-out screens mounted around the cockpit in an almost panoramic fashion.

Two men were actually flying the plane, though it looked more like they were wrestling with the controls. A flight engineer sat between them, watching over the cockpit's glut of instrumentation. Behind them taking up one side of the rear part of the flight deck were even more dials and switches; these were under the watchful eyes of two more crewmen. No TV screens, no flat panel controls, nothing fancy anywhere. Instead of headsets the five crewmen spoke to each other through ancient-looking telephones.

The girls said something to the crew in Russian. Each man looked Starr over and greeted him with a grunt.

Then one of them called out: "*Podozhdat!*"

Hang on!

Starr took his advice and grabbed the back of the engineer's seat. The huge plane went into a wide, almost sideways turn a moment later, eventually pointing its nose southwest.

They were on their way.

Chapter Two

Officially, Misha and Minky were Dima's executive assistants.

Minky spoke fair English so she offered to give him a tour of the vast airplane. She first explained that the An-225B was so mighty, it needed five of Russia's best pilots to keep it flying. On hearing this, the five shirtless men turned as one and gave Starr five thumbs-up in unison.

Minky brought him down into the cavernous cargo bay. It was really just one big long tube, more like the bottom of a sea-going freighter than something made to fly. Miles of wires and cables ran up and down its padded walls. Dreary lights burned from the ceiling. There were six large grimy wooden boxes at the very front of the bay, under the flight deck. These were the fake gas turbines the big plane was supposed to be dropping off in Johannesburg. Minky told him they were really filled with old car parts.

Taking up the rest of the cargo bay were eight bright-white modules, each the size of a small tractor-trailer, each cordoned off by strands of yellow caution tape.

One had gold lettering along its edges, setting it apart. Minky knocked twice on the door and then let Starr in.

The module contained living quarters fit for a king, or a multi-billionaire—or a rock star. Overall, it looked like an old English tavern, complete with a bar and booths, a dart board, a snooker table and two long shelves filled with dusty liquor bottles. But one wall was different. It was decorated with a couple dozen vintage guitars. Fenders, Gibsons, Les Pauls, Stratocasters, Telecasters. One neck, two-necks, even a three neck bass. They were all highly polished and beautiful, works of art themselves.

Sitting in an easy chair at the center of all this was Dima Gurtovoy. He rose as soon as Starr walked in.

Angel had described him accurately. Very tall, lanky, a Russian bookworm or professor; possibly a couple years older than Starr, closing in on thirty. Though he was well-dressed, he didn't look like $120 billion.

They shook hands and the first thing Dima said, in amusingly broken English, was: "How is my angel, Angel?"

"She's as busy as ever," Starr replied. "Hard to keep up with her sometimes."

Dima gave him a hearty pat on the back. "A pleasant problem to have." He indicated a bottle of Stoli vodka and some glasses nearby. "We must toast her . . ."

He poured out two overflowing shots and on three, they both downed them.

Dima poured two more and passed one to Starr. "I appreciate you taking on this assignment," he said. "You come highly recommended and I feel safe now that you are with us. Though I feel guilty that I am taking you away from your beautiful loved one."

"I'll see her this time tomorrow night," Starr replied. "And I'll tell her you were asking for her."

Dima raised his glass and said: *"Za zdorovye . . .* to your health."

They clinked glasses and downed the second shots.

Starr was finally warming up inside. Dima shook off the aftereffects of the eighty-proof and grinned.

"Would you like to see my collection?" he asked.

They walked back out into the cargo bay, Dima explaining that each of the pearly-white modules contained a distinct eco-system within.

Atmospheric controls, anti-vibration gear, constant monitoring by closed-circuit computers operating off AI and robotics. Everything needed to keep a high end collectible car happy during a flight half way around the world.

"These eggs alone cost a million dollars each," Dima said matter-of-factly, referring to the modules. "They're indestructible—or so they tell me."

One by one, Dima opened the first five eggs to reveal a truly magnificent car inside. This was what all the noise was about: The Dima Gurtovoy Collection.

Egg number one contained a Lamborghini Veneno.

"It means 'venom' in Spanish," Dima explained. "Only three were ever built, and I have one of them. Zero-to-60 in 2.8 seconds. $5.5 million in cash. And that was without the options . . ."

Egg number two held a 2017 Ferrari LaFerrari Aperta, which was a super futuristic looking car. "It's a tad slow," Dima explained. "It takes three seconds to reach 60 M.P.H. Price tag is $11.2 million.

A 2017 Rolls Royce Sweptail was in the third container. A one of a kind car built by the company for one of its more valued customers, it looked like a 1930s-style luxury yacht on wheels, with a roof made of one long tapered piece of glass. Price tag: $15 million.

"Number Four," Dima said, opening the next egg. "This is a 2019 Bugatti Voiture Noire, The Black Car. All carbon body, huge engine. Zero-to-60 in 2.5 seconds. Top speed 260 M.P.H. Just under $18.7 million."

But these were just play things.

The jewel of the group was in the fifth egg: a 1963 Ferrari GTO. With a design right out of the early Swinging Sixties, he called it "the Mona Lisa" of collectible cars. The price tag was a staggering: $55.5 million.

"If James Bond drove a Ferrari," Dima said. "He'd drive this car."

There were two more eggs. One contained everything needed to keep the five multi-million dollar cars running. Laser-guided diagnostic tools, banks of engine monitoring systems, spare tires, spare engines, lifts, cranks, hundreds of wrenches, screwdrivers, hammers and ratchet sets.

Dima took time to detail just about everything inside the container, clearly as proud of his tool shop as his multi-million dollar cars.

The seventh and last egg carried other things that Dima held dear, including a hundred autographed basketballs, more vintage guitars, his ultra-light sailplane, his surf boards, his mountain bikes, his collection of expensive Aldershot sausages and his extensive wardrobe. There were also a dozen wooden crates, each filled with two dozen bottles of Stolichnaya vodka.

"This will do me until I can ship the rest of my stuff," he told Starr.

The tour over, Starr was invited back to Dima's egg. It was time for breakfast.

As his bodyguard, Starr's mission was to not leave the billionaire's side until he was taken over by State Department Security at JFK and brought to Madison Square Garden to buy the Knicks. And, knowing Russians loved to talk he'd imagined there'd be a few conversations along the way.

But he wasn't prepared for this.

Once The Dima got going, the stories, the adventures, the misadventures all came rolling out of him in one long continuous monologue. Aided and abetted by Misha and Minky, whose knowing nods and occasional *skazhi eto sestra*—"tell it, sister"—served to egg him on, the billionaire brought a whole new meaning to the word gregarious.

A lot of his tales circled back around to the same topic: why Dima was leaving Russia. He had no friends in the Kremlin and the regime had made it plain they didn't like his pro-Western views or his media empire criticizing Russian leaders.

Again, the Kremlin had a habit of whacking prominent dissidents and Dima was certainly one of those. They had many methods. Staging a mugging gone bad or a fake car accident were the traditional go-tos. But the latest and most effective was to stick their victim with a poison needle or simply poison their drink.

"It's a woman's way of murdering someone," Dima told Starr. "Their method of eliminating their enemies tells you a lot about them."

He cast a glance towards Misha and Minky and shrugged.

"Beautiful creatures, yes," he whispered in English. "Trustworthy? Maybe . . ."

At this point, the two women unveiled breakfast they'd prepared themselves. It began with a Russian porridge called *kasha*, then a slice of bread topped with butter and ham, then boiled eggs, then *tvorog,* a kind of sour cottage cheese, along with some very strong tea— and, of course, a lot of vodka.

"Is all the food and drink onboard secure?" Starr asked while the small feast was brought on. As his bodyguard, this was important to know.

"We checked many times over," Dima replied. "The food . . ."

"How?" Starr wanted to know.

The Dima shrugged: "We gave some to the crew before we took off," he said. "They are still alive and seem to be feeling fine."

It was extremely crude, but Starr couldn't disagree with the method.

"How about the beverages?" he asked.

"There's no drinkable water on board for that reason," Dima replied. "We made the tea before we left and the only other thing is vodka."

Still, Starr watched the others eat, opting only for a cup of tea himself. There was some little relief that the trio in fact didn't become immediately ill, which was pretty much how most poisons worked.

"Just the five crewmen?" Starr asked. "Did you check for stowaways?"

"Yes, just them," Dima confirmed. "And the plane was under contract to us for a week before this. We searched it every day and guarded it around the clock."

He downed another shot of vodka. "As for the crewmen," he went on. "We checked their backgrounds. They're all ex-military guys, so they are not rich. When we arrive in New York, we'll be paying them more money than they've ever seen. The incentive to stay pure is the large reward at the end of the rainbow."

Starr was pleasantly surprised that Dima had taken all these precautions.

This must have shown on his face, because the billionaire added: "Lieutenant Starr—I might look like a geek or a nerd or whatever people like to call me. But I didn't make it this far by being a stupid man."

***

They passed the first few hours of the flight inside Dima's living module playing *Durak*, the national card game of Russia.

More food was brought in, and this time, Starr partook. More *Durak* followed and then Misha and Minky did some karaoke.

Finally, almost in passing, the girls confessed they knew how to read palms and a fortune-telling session began.

They read each other's palms first, coming up with predictions such as: You will soon have a long journey—with a lot of sunshine at the end.

Dima good-naturedly agreed to be next. His fortune was just as predictable: "You will distribute your great wealth among your small circle of best friends," and "You know how to drive in luxury . . ."

Then it was Starr's turn. Again just in an effort to pass the time, he surrendered to the two beauties. Misha took his hand, looked at his palm—but then froze.

She looked at Minky, and literally put Starr's palm in her's. The joviality had vanished. Suddenly, it was dead serious inside the egg.

Finally Misha looked him in the eye and said: "You will soon learn some very bad news . . ."

And at that moment, Starr's odd brand of ESP kicked in.

And all he could say was: "I think you're right . . ."

He decided to stay outside Dima's egg for the remainder of the flight.

It would put him in a better position to protect the billionaire, though he didn't know who on board the plane could possibly do him harm.

Piloting the winged mammoth was a full time job; the plane sometimes flew with as many as eight in the cockpit. None of the present flight crew could go missing for any amount of time without his absence being noticed. Of course, there was always a chance the five men were in on something together. But again Dima's people checked them out, plus they were flying towards a very big payday if all went according to plan. While anything was possible, they were unlikely potential suspects.

Misha and Minky? Starr couldn't imagine the two beautiful assistants as assassins either. It was clear they were both enthralled, if not in love, with Dima. He could see them doing bodily harm to anyone who might threaten the billionaire, but definitely not the other way around.

Still, Starr took to searching the cavernous hold every hour on the hour only because it made him feel better to be doing something. The dull lights, the steamy heat and the bumpy ride all made for a unique kind of unpleasant-ness; plus the hold was full of dark shadows and strange noises. But there really was nowhere for anyone to hide. The eggs were triple-locked and secure. He'd checked each of the fake gas turbine crates with every hourly pass. They were indeed crammed with fenders and bumpers and the heat alone would make anyone hiding inside want to surrender.

He had an attachment for his NightVision goggles which allowed him a kind of super-hearing. It was directional and controllable so he could tune out the normal if weird in-flight sounds, sweep the plane, and hear things like people breathing or hands moving quietly. But there were only eight others on board and he knew where they all were. Beyond all that, he heard nothing out of the ordinary. He also had a Sniffer with him; it could detect odors associated with explosives down to one particle in a million. He never turned it off and it had yet to make a beep.

So, the plane was clean. There were no bombs, no plausible suspects, no assassins hiding onboard.

Then why was his ESP flashing that the billionaire's life was in imminent danger?

Chapter Three

It was ten minutes before midnight when they began their final approach to Johannesburg Airport.

Starr returned to the gold-embroidered egg and had a heart-to-heart talk with Dima. His advice: he and the billionaire should get off the flight in Johannesburg and quietly make other arrangements to get to New York.

"Call it instinct or whatever," Starr told him. "But I think it's best we switch aircraft here, proceed to New York by another means. I will stay at your side until the State Department security guys take over at JFK. I'll wait for the An-225B to arrive and re-fuel at JFK and then I'll hitch a ride on it to Arizona where I promise I'll personally see to it that every car is safe in its new digs."

But Dima was taken aback by the suggestion.

"Why?" he wanted to know. "We've been nothing but safe so far. Food is good, drink is good. No one is questioning what's actually aboard this plane. Plus we went over every square inch of the aircraft before take-off and found nothing to endanger us. And you've been doing nothing but searching for ghosts ever since."

Starr couldn't disagree with him. The plane was absolutely clean. Yet the feeling that something was about to go wrong would not let him go.

"I was told you have some kind of sixth sense," Dima went on. "But I didn't know if it was true or not."

"It's true," Starr admitted. "And it's not wrong too often. And at the moment, it's telling me to at least have this conversation with you."

Dima never stopped smiling. "And I thought Russians were superstitious."

Starr shrugged. He was uncomfortable talking about the subject, but he had to give the billionaire some sort of explanation for his radical change in plans.

"I have to say it has nothing to do with superstition," he replied quietly.

"Then that settles it," Dima said with a clap of his hands. "Nothing will happen to us because we've already thought about it too much and that's how the Cosmos works. Too much thinking about it makes it all go away."

Johannesburg Airport was soaking wet and foggy.

They touched down at exactly midnight in the middle of a torrential rain storm.

The giant bird creaked and groaned the last few hundred feet down, hitting the ground with the violence of a moderate car crash.

It used the airport's entire extended runway and took fifteen minutes to turn around and rumble its way back to the cargo terminal.

The ground crew was in Dima's employ. They went through the charade of off-loading the fake turbine crates, and then the plane's fuel tanks were topped off.

About the same time, though, Dima heard from a source in Moscow that the Kremlin was aware of his defection, which was no surprise. But the billionaire was flatly unworried.

"We just have to fly one last leg of this journey," he told Starr as they waited for the big plane to finish gassing-up. "Then all will be well."

Starr prevailed in one request. He asked Dima to turn his faux ground crew into security guards and have them ring the An-225B while it was on the ground to make sure no one could get near it to do any harm. He also checked that the fuel being on-loaded came from the same source as all the other planes refueling at the airport.

Starr *also* insisted on searching the big airplane one more time before leaving Johannesburg. It took him a half hour to check any and all possible places someone could put a bomb—but again, he found nothing.

They finally took off again at 2 A.M. Forty five minutes behind schedule, they headed northwest, towards the United States, sixteen hours away.

Chapter Four

Starr was an expert at staying awake for long stretches of time.

It came with the job. Special operations rarely ran nine-to-five on weekdays with weekends off. More often they took place at the most ungodly hours and seemed to go on forever. Being able to stay awake to work the mission was a big plus.

But Starr wouldn't have been able to go to sleep if he'd tried. His unusual brand of short-term ESP hadn't stopped flashing since the palm reading session in Dima's Egg, telling him some kind of danger was imminent.

It *was* strange. Usually, he would get these precognitions in quick bursts. Two or three seconds ahead, just enough to duck a punch, and then it would be over.

But this particular premonition had been pulsating inside him for hours—and it was driving him crazy. He took to walking up and down the entire length of the huge cargo hold non-stop, checking places he'd checked many times before. In between every other trip he'd climb up to the flight deck and check in with the shirtless crew.

None of them spoke English, or just chose not to, so he'd simply give them a thumbs-up with a quizzical look on his face and the crew would always report back with five uplifted thumbs of their own. Still, it did little to ease his concerns.

The noise and the relentless heat didn't help his well-being either. He'd faced this kind of situation before. A deep psychic hole, the answer down there somewhere, just out of reach. But whenever he was out of possible solutions, whenever he needed an objective point of view, there was one person he could always call . . .

His secret weapon.

Angel.

He'd hesitated this time, though. After what they'd just gone through with the Father Friendly case, they'd agreed to cool it when it came to talking to each other on the obsolete satellite phones they called the Tomato Cans.

But though rare, these psychic headaches of his could persist unless he unloaded on somebody—and that was always her. He couldn't perform to the best of his ability while under this kind of duress.

So for the sake of the mission, he quietly retrieved his Tomato Can from his gray camouflage gig bag and walked to the very end of the huge cargo bay.

He activated its power supply, folded out the tiny satellite dish and entered the 22-digit pass code. Then he punched in the number of Angel's Tomato Can.

There was always some anxiety when he did this. First, he'd get concerned if she didn't answer right away. Second, he was always worried that instead of talking to Angel, he'd suddenly be talking to a Navy security officer who'd finally found out what they'd been doing with the elderly communicators.

To his great delight, she answered on the first beep.

"I was so hoping you'd call," she said in full Angel-mode. "I rely on this so much to make sure you're okay. So . . . are you okay?"

"Yes, I am, are you?"

She was.

He told her where he was and what he was doing—and the reason for the dread that kept creeping up on him.

"I've searched this plane fifty times on my own," he said. "And Dima's security forces searched it and sanitized it before it left Moscow. The food is not poisoned. There's no water on board and I checked the refueling fuel myself. Add in the fact that these things are usually done with the prick of a needle—and it just doesn't make sense then that I'm getting this . . . you know, message from beyond."

She was quiet for a moment. Starr could almost hear her thinking.

"I can only tell you what you always tell me," she said finally. "When something like this is nagging at you, don't go nuts trying to figure out what's wrong with you and instead concentrate on how your vision might come true, no matter how crazy it is . . ."

And that's when it happened. By her words alone a final piece fell into place and he realized at last what it was he'd been uneasy about.

"I've got to go, honey," he told her. "Please stay safe and I'll call you as soon as I can."

They exchanged I-love-you's and said goodbye.

Then he ran back to the cargo bay where the eggs were kept, found Dima and the two girls and said: "We are going to crash soon. Go up to the flight deck and get prepared . . ."

Chapter Five

Namacunde, Angola

The small airfield had been built by the Cubans back in 1980.

It was literally in the middle of the jungle. But it was big enough, especially its runway, to handle jet aircraft.

While the Angolan air force had jet fighters, most were elderly and chronically out of service. However, they maintained their installations to the point where fighters from other countries could land there in secret.

That's what was happening at Namacunde today.

The two fighter jets had arrived during the monsoon-like rain storm that swept the bottom of the African continent all that night.

They'd landed on the single long runway, hurriedly taxied back to the pair of concrete shelters and quickly got out of sight.

Both were Russian-built Su-34 fighter-bombers, both were manned by two-person Russian crews, but the Russian Air Force markings had been removed and Syrian Air Force emblems put on instead.

No one at the small airfield had any idea why.

The Su-34 was unusual in a number of ways. It was gigantic for a fighter plane and was actually more like a small bomber. It also had extremely long range, thanks to lots of internal fuel capacity as well as the ability to carry large drop tanks under its wings.

This was what the Su-34 was designed for, ultra-long missions of 2,000 miles or more. It was the perfect airplane for what lay afoot.

There they stayed, in their concrete hiding places, serviced by a small team of Angolan ground personnel, waiting for the hours to pass.

Midnight came and went. The rain continued and the wind was picking up over the ocean and blowing in towards shore.

At 2:05A.M., the airfield received a message from somewhere in the Middle East. It contained a single word: "Launch . . ."

Within five minutes both big fighter jets were back on the runway, their two-man crews arming their gigantic nose mounted cannons. The rain started coming down even harder, but it made no difference. The Su-34 was not only built for long range combat, it was able to fly any kind of weather.

When all was ready, the pilots hit their throttles and were off. Rising into the stormy night, they immediately headed southwest.

Chapter Six

Starr knew they were coming.

Two of them, flying out of the north.

Big planes . . .

Heading right for the An-225B.

They rocketed by them just a few seconds later, showing up on the cargo plane's rudimentary radar screen as two massive blips moving very fast.

Their arrival made a weird kind of sense though. It was night, they were battling a never-ending rain storm, over a pretty wild part of southwest Africa.

It was the perfect place for an ambush.

But Starr was prepared and so were the rest of the plane's occupants. His precognition skills had told him to gather everyone into the aircraft's safest place: the flight deck.

If the big plane was going down, this is where you want to be.

They could see the two jets now, but only by their nose lights and the flare from their rear exhaust tubes. They looked surreal, though; crazy lights blazing across the sky, unaffected by the driving rains.

Starr told Minky to tell everyone else to strap in. They needed no prompting; everyone started buckling their seat belts and safety harnesses. No sooner were they done when they saw the lights of the two fighter jets turn one-eighty and start back towards the big plane.

The An-225B's lead pilot flipped down his Night-Vision glasses and rattled off two sentences in deep Russian. Huddled on the flight deck next to Starr, Minky translated for him: "He said, 'These are Russian planes. They are here to harass us only.' "

No sooner were those words out of his mouth when the two jets rocketed by them again, crossing over the An-225B's big nose. This violently disrupted the air flow in front of it, causing the winged giant to weave out of control for a few hairy seconds, before the pilots regained flight.

The two jets disappeared low and to their starboard side. Any last question that these might be interceptors from some African country was dispelled when the An-225B's engineer was able to find the operating radio frequency of the two planes and heard nothing but guttural Russian.

"*Oni vozvrashchayutsya!*" he cried. "They are coming back . . ."

The two jets buzzed the An-225B once again, coming so close, the mammoth cargo plane shook from one end to the other, rocked by twin shock waves and the resulting turbulence. The noise was tremendous.

This time the jets were wagging their wings, an unspoken rule of the air which meant: "Follow me . . ."

But the An-225B's pilots were having none of that.

When the fighters screamed by for a fourth time, the An-225B pilots snapped on their flight deck lights, allowing the Su-34 pilots to look right inside the beast and see them displaying a wide range of graphically obscene gestures.

Starr shouted a warning to the pilots, translated by Minky, telling them to cool it. But it was too late.

They heard another loud roar—this time it was the sound of the Su-34s' nose cannons. In two quick bursts from each plane, half of the An-225B's enormous tail section was shot away.

Suddenly the pilots were fighting their controls as the big plane began to falter. Everything inside was shaking now and it seemed like they were going to roll over at any moment. Only through pure muscle power did the pilots manage to get them level again.

But tail section damage was usually catastrophic. It might take a while for the stresses on the rest of the aircraft to come into play, but eventually it was going to cause a crash. It was just a matter of where and when.

The two Su-34s circled back, and roared across the nose of the big plane yet again. One of the fighter pilots gave them a mocking wave as they went by. He too knew the An-225B was mortally wounded. He too knew what came next was inevitable.

This really infuriated the An-225B pilots. When the two jets went by again, the pilots let loose with every graphic and pornographic gesture that they knew.

It was a Russian thing, curse your killer to the end.

But the Su-34s pilots were Russian too.

So they came back for a final time. Rocketing by the nose once again, the lead jet fired its cannon directly into the cockpit, killing both pilots instantly.

Two seconds later, the big airplane started going down.

Chapter Seven

As an offshoot to his short-term precognition ability, Starr was sometimes able to slow down time itself.

Or that's what it felt like.

The Navy scientists eventually figured out what was happening: he was actually remembering things very, very quickly—unique frontal lobe meta-synapsing—and that gave him the illusion that things were slowing down.

These episodes never lasted very long so he'd learned to take advantage of them when they happened.

It was a moment after the plane's pilots had been killed and the plane started to go out of control that time almost came to a halt for him. Suddenly he was inside a movie, moving at a super slow motion. All the lights had gone out, the plane's cockpit was full of holes and the rain and wind were blowing in. The two pilots were shot to pieces and lying bloody across the controls. The noise was tremendous.

Only one thought occurred to him: What would be the smartest thing to do in this moment?

The answer came in a flash. Fighting the increasing g-forces, he glided into the cockpit, somehow found the plane's auto-pilot switch and punched it.

His action abruptly pulled the An-225B out of its dive, unleashing an ear-splitting mechanical growl in the process. Another flash and Starr was back in real time again.

But he was immediately disbelieving what he'd done.

"Nothing's that easy . . ." he whispered.

He was right. A moment later the big plane started yawing to the left; suddenly it was like they were flying sideways. Starr pulled one of the dead pilots out of his seat and climbed into it himself. He tried to jam down the foot pedals for the plane's elevators, hoping to right the plane, but this time, the competing aerodynamics were just too great.

Yet once again, just as it seemed they were doomed, the big plane suddenly, miraculously, began flying straight again.

What happened? Through the rain and fire and smoke, Starr saw the flight engineer—the third man up front—had slid into the co-pilot's seat next to him and with his help they'd been able to move the elevators enough to bring the plane's nose back to center again.

But they were still going down, just not as fast.

Starr looked over at the man.

"English?" Starr yelled.

"Nay mnogo!" was the shouted reply, meaning not much. *"Russkiy?"*

Starr shook his head. "Not enough to do what we've got to do . . ."

He yelled back to Minky; they needed a translator. She climbed up into the dark, smoky cockpit, now rattling so much it seemed like it would come apart at any moment. Sparks were flying from the control panel, the wind was whipping through holes made by the cannon shells. Fires were breaking out all around them— and they were once again losing altitude fast.

Nevertheless, Minky was able to pull both dead pilots out of the cockpit and then squeezed herself in between Starr and the flight engineer.

"Please tell him my name is Chris," Starr said to her. She did as asked and then told him: "He is Boris . . ."

Boris reached over and shook Starr's hand.

He said: *"Davay sdelayem eto . . ."*

Translated by Minky: "Let's do this thing . . ."

Starr replied: "We fly it until the last part stops moving, okay?"

Boris nodded with vigor and said, *"Poslednyaya budet ya . . ."*

Rough translation: "The last part moving will be me . . ."

The attack had taken place at 40,000 feet. By now they were at 20,000 feet and still dropping. The big plane had been moving all over the sky since dealing with the

Su-34s; they had no idea where they were or what they were going to hit.

But as this was southwest Africa, the chances of slamming into a mountain were very, very good. Mount Goboboseb or any peak in the Great Kara range—take your pick. When planes crashed in this part of Africa, they frequently impacted on mountains.

Even if they were lucky enough to miss all the mountains, and were able to come in somewhat level, they would still be facing an extremely violent crash. The An-225B itself weighed more than 600,000 pounds empty. That would be a lot of mass coming down with a lot of momentum.

Another concern: the An-225B loaded and unloaded from the front. Unlike just about every other cargo plane ever built, there was no rear door. So when the crash came, everything inside the cargo bay would keep moving forward, burst through the loading doors and go flying out of the nose.

This was not good news for Dima's car collection, but worse, it could cause the plane to topple nose over tail, and that would be the end of all of them, for sure.

At 15,000 feet and now dropping faster, Starr started calling out things they needed to do to prepare for the imminent crash.

"Dump fuel," he yelled. Minky translated and with the push of three buttons, Boris purged 95-percent of their remaining fuel. The airplane immediately felt lighter, but it was still falling from the sky.

"Remove all glasses!" Starr called out. "Takeoff high heels, take off all belts . . ."

The girls, the remaining crew members and Dima immediately complied.

"Tighten safety straps!" Starr yelled. Then he leaned over to Minky and added: "You too."

The plane was at 5,000 feet now, dropping into the pitch black, rain pelting it with a sound similar to bullet rounds. The g-forces were getting unbearable.

Four thousand feet . . .

If they were going to hit a mountain, now would be the time. His legs numb as he and Boris continued to battle the plane's elevators Starr closed his eyes and waited . . .

Is this it? he thought.

But nothing happened. When he opened them again, they were still flying, but still descending very fast.

Down through 3,000 feet, 2,000, then 1,000. The rain clouds were extra thick now; they couldn't see anything beyond the nose. Even hitting a smaller mountain would spell disaster for them at this point, as would crashing into dense jungle, the kind that would cover them up in a day, hiding everything from above forever.

But neither was to be.

They broke through the cloud layer at 800 feet and by the sheer light of their burning wings they saw they were over a desert—one with mountainous sand dunes.

Starr only had enough time to yell over to Minky: "Tell everyone to brace for impact!"

She did so and then put her head down, and held it in her hands.

The big plane slammed into the ground two seconds later.

Chapter Eight

Orange dust . . .

That was the first thing that registered in Starr's brain. Lots of orange dust, filling the cockpit.

He thought it was blood spray at first, but actually it was the plane's nose disintegrating. Metal, wires, rubber, foam padding, glass, plastic, tons of electronics, all of it magically turning to a fine orange mist on impact. It made it hard to breathe. The oxygen around him was burning up.

In the next moment, the front of the big plane was torn open and the eight egg modules came flying out, tumbling away like some giant's toys.

Still the plane continued careening across the sand, losing more and more of itself along the way. Weakened by the fire, the right wing broke off causing them to spin. But then the left wing crumpled and fell away and suddenly the plane wasn't spinning anymore, but back to plowing straight ahead. But it seemed to go on forever.

After another quarter mile, they finally came to a bone-crunching, banshee-screeching stop. The flight deck separated from the rest of the airplane and was flung away. What was left of the An-225B burst into flames.

That was Starr's last memory of the crash itself—the flight deck flying through the air, as he was, still strapped to his seat. He was hit by something while airborne, something hard, square on his melon.

He blacked out after that.

He woke up in Hell.

Lying face down in the sand, he lifted his head to see he was in a forest of burning, twisted wreckage.

It was raining hard, the wind was blowing ferocious-ly and the sand felt like shards of glass hitting his face. Yet gigantic pieces of the airplane were on fire all around him; thousands of pieces of smaller debris were every-where too. Plastic, rubber, metal; nothing bigger than a fist, all of it smoking or on fire. Large and small, this was all he could see in every direction.

But it was even more bizarre than that.

Dozens of basketballs were also bouncing around the debris, the wet, swirling wind blowing them everywhere. Miles of electrical wire were entangled in everything including both his legs. Bottles of vodka were scattered everywhere, too—some smashed, some just charred—as were hundreds of large sausages. Meanwhile, long pieces of yellow caution tape were slithering through the air like aerial snakes.

But strangest of all: Money, and pieces of money, was also flying around. U.S. currency, mostly $500 bills, hundreds of them blowing in the wind.

"I'm dead," he thought, because what he was seeing just didn't seem real. "I'm actually dead . . ."

But then . . . above the fierce wind and rain, the blowing sand and the roar of flames, he heard a voice crying out: "*Navakhu!*"

Up here . . .

Starr looked up and saw what was left of the flight compartment hanging ten feet above him—upside down.

Still strapped in her seat, while everything else around her had been blown away in the crash, was Minky. She was waving a small flashlight down at him, almost casually, as if she'd been doing it for a while, which she had.

"Thank you for finally looking my way!" she shouted down to him.

"Undo your belt and I'll catch you!" he yelled up to her.

And that's exactly what she did. No confirmation, no here-I-come. She just unbuckled and next thing he knew she was coming down fast. He braced just in time to catch her in his arms and stop her fall—but then they both toppled to the ground.

He recovered and crawled over to her. She looked dead or at least unconscious. He lifted her gently from her shoulders.

"Are you okay?" he pleaded with her. "Please be okay . . ."

She suddenly opened her eyes and then stuck the flashlight in his face, blinding him.

"Do you know how long I was hanging up there?" she scolded him.

He was so glad she was alive he actually kissed her on the top of the head. Then he got her to her feet.

Now for the first time, she was able to take in her surroundings too. Minky was a tough cookie—that was obvious—but this affected her. The sheer amount of wreckage and flames was unreal. Huge fires were all around them despite the downpour. Add in basketballs, caution tape, five hundred dollar bills. Smashed guitars and sausages everywhere, with a smell like spilled gasoline and sewage.

"My God, it *is* Hell," she said.

He led her out from underneath the dangling piece of wreckage and about fifty feet away from the remains of the big plane's flight compartment. But it did little to change the scenery.

The airplane's remains were spread out in a massive debris field; it looked at least a half mile around. And even the sand was on fire in many places.

That's when it hit her. "Oh my God," she said. "We're the only ones left? We're the only ones who survived?"

It seemed that way . . . for about five seconds.

Then they heard more voices off to their left. Out of the twisting smoke and sand, Starr spotted Boris, the flight engineer who'd brought the plane in with him. Still shirtless, his chest hair was seared and still smoldering in some places.

But other than that, he didn't look hurt or very concerned, for that matter.

He was carrying a smashed and empty vodka bottle. He walked up to them and asked in Russian: "You two okay?"

They vigorously assured him they were, even trying a sort of half embrace to show him they were glad he was still alive.

But Boris had other things on his mind.

"Dima's vodka," he said, eyes sweeping the sands. "Is everywhere . . ."

With that, he half-staggered away.

"That's sad," Starr said, convinced Boris was in a state of shock.

But Minky set him straight. "He's always like that," she said.

Then, more voices.

They helped each other around a large part of the wrecked fuselage and here they found Dima, the two other crewmen and Misha.

She was hurt; the others were huddled around her.

Dima was happy to see them, at least. He hugged both tight.

"I am so glad you're alive," he told them, in tears. "This is all my fault. This was a stupid idea from the beginning."

Minky had her way. She slapped him, hard. "You're not a girl, Dima" she said. "Stop acting like one . . ."

Then she looked at her friend on the ground.

"What happened to her?" she asked.

His face still smarting, Dima pulled them aside, out of earshot.

"Both arms broken," he told them, adding: "In multiple places . . ."

Starr went back and knelt beside Misha. He didn't need to be a doctor to know Dima was right. The beautiful blonde girl had fractures up and down both arms.

She was calm though.

For the moment.

Dima was suddenly next to him.

"What do we do, Lieutenant? I'm hoping you will know . . ."

Starr looked around. They had to at least get Misha to some shelter.

But where?

The return of Boris solved the problem. Once again, he came out of the smoke and wind, this time his arms full of unbroken vodka bottles. He waved to the small group indicating they should follow him.

Dima and Starr gingerly lifted Misha to her feet. The two crewmen—they were Stan and Oleg—then scooped her up by her bottom and very carefully began carrying her, following Boris's footsteps.

They all made their way down from the major part of the debris field to a large sand bowl where one of the eggs had come to rest.

Unlike the others, it hadn't crumpled on impact. Rather it tumbled end over end for more than 100 yards before coming to a stop on its roof. Boris had found it previously and partially forced its door open.

It was the egg that had contained the 2017 Rolls Royce Sweptail. It had tumbled for nearly a quarter mile crushing the $17-million car inside beyond all recognition.

When they fully opened both its doors, a few hundred loose pieces of what used to be the very high end car spilled out on them. What was left still attached to the chassis looked as if it had been battered by a giant fist. An auto-crushing machine couldn't have done a better job.

Dima started crying again. While he could afford to buy a thousand other cars just as valuable, as he put it, this car had been a work of art.

But the container itself was still in one piece, and fairly level. Boris, Stan and Oleg quickly cleared a space near the door and lay Misha down very gently on a bed of large pieces of foam-rubber insulation that were also blowing around everywhere. The interior of the egg smelled heavily of gasoline, and the rain was coming in through some cracks in what was now its roof.

But it was shelter. So the rest crowded inside, closed the doors and tended to their wounds as best they could—all by flashlight.

Outside, the wind and rain only grew worse.

Chapter Nine

Starr remembered thinking, if this had been a movie, all of the survivors inside the egg would have passed out from exhaustion and gone to sleep.

But this was not a movie.

And no one slept.

During the next few hours, no one stayed in one place either, except Misha, laid out on the foam rubber and Starr, who stayed in place next to the bent and crumpled doors.

Everyone else—Minky, Boris, the two other crewmen, Stan and Oleg, and especially Dima—couldn't sit still in one place for more than a few minutes before having to move to yet another place inside the crowded egg. It was like a certain kind of restlessness was built into all of them. But all the unsettling and moving around made a bad situation worse.

The spell was broken only when Stan and Oleg ventured outside into the fierce storm, which they did three times during the night, their only flashlight in hand. They never came back empty handed though. Vodka bottles and sausages were scattered everywhere, they'd become expert in collecting them. This allowed Boris to feed

Misha a steady diet of Stoli, nobly easing her situation as best he could.

Still, the hours dragged on. Starr stayed at his post until finally he saw through a crack in the doors that the sky was brightening. Dawn was not far away.

That's when Dima came over and sat beside him. He whispered, "What do we do now, Lieutenant?"

It was a great question—but Starr didn't have an answer.

Their flight, at least officially, was off the books. Everyone in Russia had been paid off; the same was true in Johannesburg. The plane, the crew, the cargo did not exist. So what country was going to launch a rescue mission for a flight that never happened?

Plus, they'd flown almost the entire way under radio silence. Those waiting for them in the U.S. knew this and weren't expecting to hear from them until they were approaching U.S. airspace. That was still hours from now.

Even then, when they didn't show up, it would take some time to get the wheels turning to see what went wrong. And that search would have to start back in Moscow—and they were a long way from Russia at the moment.

"The biggest problem," Starr told him, "is that the only people who know where we are, approximately, are the ones who shot us down. They're probably not going to trigger an all-out search and rescue. I think our only hope is that someone flying nearby sees the wreckage. We're somewhere in Africa, people are flying around all the time. And that was a large debris field."

At that moment, the wind blew the doors wide open, and the sunshine poured in. Dima looked over Starr's shoulder to the desert beyond.

His face fell a mile.

"That is no longer our biggest problem," he said dourly.

Starr turned and looked out at the desert.

He could see no wreckage. He could barely see out the doors. The wind and sand had already covered over most of the debris field.

"No one's going to see us now," Dima said, once more almost in tears. "No one's going to ever see us again . . ."

Chapter Ten

It took Starr fifteen minutes to climb out of the sand bowl.

One thing not distorted by the craziness following the crash was that some of the sand dunes around him really *were* as tall as small skyscrapers. So it was a long slow ascent, climbing in the thin, fine, almost powder-like sand, with the morning growing warmer by the second.

Finally reaching the summit, he looked back into the sand bowl and could barely see the smashed egg where he'd left the others. Even from this height, little of the debris field remained visible.

This troubled him greatly. If he had a hard time making out the crash site from here, how would anyone flying overhead ever spot them?

He walked along the top of the dune. The sky was clear and the morning sun was blazing by now, but the wind was still blowing fiercely. The billions of pieces of sand all moving at once made a sound of its own, almost a deep groaning noise.

But still, above all that, Starr heard something else.

Waves, crashing . . .

He hiked over to the next dune, taking ten minutes to navigate the narrow slippery spine that connected the two. Once there, he looked west and not a half mile away he saw the ocean, and indeed giant waves were crashing against its shore. Some of them were so high their chicanes seemed to stretch for miles.

Though it was a perfectly clear weather, this part of the sea looked like it had been roiled by a hurricane. There was not a cloud in the sky, no big storms out on the horizon. Yet the water here was incredibly rough, the height of some waves near nightmarish proportions.

One thing was brutally clear. Had they stayed aloft just a few seconds longer, they would have crashed into this angry sea—and none of them would have survived.

He looked north and south, and saw nothing but the treacherous shoreline running for miles in both directions. To his back was a hostile-looking desert that also stretched on forever. Yet, looking back towards the shore, he saw a number of wildlife down near the water, including several packs of elephants.

It slowly started to come together. The high-dune desert. The winds. The monstrous waves. The animal life close-by.

Suddenly, he knew where they were. The desert coast of Namibia, one of the most inhospitable parts of Africa—and one of the worst places on Earth to be lost.

Hundreds of ships, airplanes, and people had met their end in this place over the centuries. It was so remote, so treacherous, anyone stranded here had an excellent chance of being lost forever.

Or at least until they turned into bones.

That's why they called it The Skeleton Coast.

It took a lot less time for Starr to get off the dune.

One, two, three running steps and gravity took over. He started sliding at first, but then increased speed and momentum and began tumbling. It was something a kid might like, but he wasn't a kid anymore. By the time he reached the bottom he felt he'd been pummeled more than during the plane crash.

He made his way back to the shelter egg, but only Minky and Misha were inside. They were trading shots of vodka, keeping the pain level down for the injured girl.

Minky didn't even look up when he came in. She just waved over her shoulder and said: "They're all out back . . ."

Starr grabbed a half sausage from the pile near the door; it was about the size of a cucumber. He brushed off as much sand as he could and started devouring it, at the same time taking a long swig of vodka from one of the dozens of unbroken bottles Boris had found in the sand.

"Breakfast of Champions." he murmured.

Boris, Stan and Oleg had built an improvised tent out back. They'd used various bits of fabric found in the sand around the buried crash site for the top and they'd repurposed some narrow turbine blades from the An-225B's jet engines as the poles. The tent was about eight feet high, had four retractable sides, and covered an area of about fifty square feet. It provided some relief from the now-broiling sun.

But this wasn't built strictly for comfort.

Starr went inside and saw that the Russian crewmen were collecting salvage from the remains of the An-225B and storing it in the tent. Smashed guitars, basketballs, the remains of Dima's million-dollar sail plane, actuators from the various car wrecks, even a few dozen crumpled $500 bills.

Starr was both surprised and intrigued. He walked up beside Dima.

"They're having a yard sale?" he asked the billion-aire.

Dima just shrugged. "If it keeps them busy . . ."

Starr told him what he'd seen from the top of the nearby dune. Dima's face turned pale. He knew of the Skeleton Coast.

They moved out of the tent, leaving the crewmen to their devices.

"My God," Dima exclaimed once they'd walked some distance away. "Could we have crashed in a worse place?"

Starr pointed to the west. "The ocean is just over the big dune," he said. "Landing in that would have been worse."

Dima scanned the clear skies above. "We'd look like bugs to anyone flying over us," he said. "And I'm sure no one flies over this place very often anyway—not with its bad reputation."

"We *are* in a challenging position," Starr confessed. "There's no way to get word out to anybody. And from what I saw from the top of the dunes, we can't walk out of here. There's nothing around for what seems like hundreds of miles."

Dima's 7'2" body immediately became hunched, the pained look back on his face.

"All my fault," he said again. "My stupid idea. We all would have been better off if we did crash into the ocean, because at least it would have been over. Now we're doomed to die out here, slow and alone."

Starr knew despondency could be contagious.

So he said: "My suggestion is, we gather as much flammable material as we can find or dig up easily and we build a bonfire, up on that dune. Light it up tonight, see what happens."

Dima's face brightened. It was a simple plan, but enough to perk up his spirits. He straightened out his lanky frame.

"Another reason I'm glad you're here," he said, clapping Starr on the back. "Let's do it."

Chapter Eleven

That became their day.

Dima, Starr and Minky canvassed what they could still see of the vast debris field, looking for things they could light on fire.

But their mission quickly turned into a full-scale salvaging operation as they began finding things valuable to their present situation. This included a fifty gallon tank of distilled water that was used as part of the giant airplane's engine cooling system. It had survived the crash with little more than a few dents and Starr deemed it unlikely to be poisoned.

They also found larger and cleaner pieces of foam for Misha to lie on, a hand drill, a hammer and lots of intact vodka bottles. And lots of sausages.

It took them all day, in the brutal sun, but they did it without complaint, each knowing that in light of their dire circumstances, it was best to keep busy and to work towards a goal.

They became somewhat expert at it too.

Though ninety percent of the debris field had been covered by the blowing sand, in some places the covering was only a few inches deep. They found these places by listening carefully as they walked, waiting to hear a tell-tale crunching sound indicating there was something right below.

Walking three abreast about twenty feet apart, once something was found, they would converge on the site and start to dig with their bare hands. Sometimes it was just a pile of crushed aircraft materials or balls of burned electronics.

But other times they found things like blankets, tools, and a box full of cigarette lighters and, maybe best of all, packages of chewing gum.

While moving their finds inside the survival egg and making things more comfortable for Misha, they'd also amassed a large pile of flammable materials at the bottom of the grand dune. The plan was to start carrying them up to the peak once the sun began setting and the ruthless heat would become a little bit less so.

They decided a station to station process would be the best. Minky would carry some material about half way of the dune, where she'd leave it in a pile. Dima would then haul it to the top of the dune, where Starr would then carry it to the very peak where the bonfire was planned.

As soon as the sun started to dip, they set this plan in motion.

Starr made the initial ascent, carrying a dozen pieces of wood that came from the paneling of Dima's demolished Rolls. He also had two pockets full of cigarette lighters and two full vodka bottles to serve as the accelerant.

His plan was to get the fire going, walk down to Dima's pile, bring up additional materials, keep building it and get the biggest fire going as possible.

Would it help?

He doubted it. They might as well be at the North Pole or someplace equally isolated.

But, considering their circumstances, it couldn't hurt.

At least, he didn't think so.

Within an hour, the sun was gone and his fire was blazing away.

As it turned out he didn't need much of the vodka to help get it going. Most of the debris was soaked with aviation fuel. So he drank some of the vodka instead.

He would usually see Dima from far away; when the billionaire would drop off more materials, Starr would walk down to retrieve them. By that time, Dima was already on his way down.

So Starr was alone for long stretches of time. Just he and the fire and the frightening situation he found himself in.

Angel . . .

He knew he would probably never see her again. He'd been in tight spots before, but never had this particular thought crossed his mind so vividly, so conclusively.

He looked out over the turbulent Atlantic, as if he could see America somewhere far beyond. He'd have to see across another entire continent after that, because she was home in San Diego, expecting him to call soon to tell her the Dima mission was complete and he was heading home.

Now, she'd never get that call.

And she'd never know what happened to him.

Feeling dreadfully down about his fate, thinking what the end was going to be like, he drank most of the vodka he should have been throwing on the fire. How long he sat here like this, he didn't know.

But at some point . . . he thought he heard something.

A cross between a buzz and a beep. Very electronic, but very familiar, too.

He had to stop his head from spinning and try to filter out the rush of the wind and the crackle of the fire to concentrate on what he thought he was hearing.

That sound?

It was impossible . . .

The next thing he knew, he was running down the side of the enormous dune, half-full vodka bottle in hand. Tripping, falling, getting to his feet again, he had to get back to the enormous debris field as fast as he could.

He started tumbling about half way down. This was how he passed Dima, nearly knocking down Minky once he got to the bottom.

He half ran past the tent behind the shelter egg; the front flap was open and he could see the three Russian crewmen were still in there, hunched over something, drunkenly singing some very Russian-sounding song. They barely acknowledged him as he hurried by.

It was nearly pitch black down here, the little light there was coming from a half dozen small fires still burning themselves out. Starr found an empty vodka bottle, stuffed some stray insulation into it and lit it. Now he had a torch.

The wind was absolutely howling and the Russian crewmen continued their singing and he could even hear the waves crashing onto the shore nearby.

But he could also still hear that faint sound.

Almost hypnotic.

Buzz, beep.

Buzz, beep.

He wound up stumbling around the covered-over debris field for more than an hour. Drinking steadily, now close to very drunk, yet never stopping in his quest.

But then he suddenly froze—and just listened. At that moment, the mysterious noise sounded like it was coming from many different directions at once.

He threw the vodka bottle away, almost in a panic, frightened he was going mad so soon.

But then he looked down at his feet, and lit by the torch, he could see a small section of the sand was moving, dozens of grains bouncing up into the air for no apparent reason.

He was instantly on his hands and knees and digging madly.

It seemed to take forever, but about three feet down he hit pay dirt.

He first saw a patch of gray camouflage pattern. It was stained with some kind of hydraulic fluid, but he would have known it anywhere.

It was his gig bag.

He dug more madly now, clearing enough sand away to unzip the top.

Buzz, beep . . .

Buzz, beep . . .

The noise was so loud now, it sounded like it was echoing through a massive sound system and into his ears.

He reached inside the bag, his fingers trembling as they made their way through his stuff, straining to get to the very bottom.

Then, suddenly he found it, squeezed it and quickly took it out.

It was his Tomato Can.

And it was ringing.

His hands were shaking so much he had a hard time opening the strange sat-phone's cover, unfolding the tiny antenna and hitting the receive button.

"Angel . . ." he half yelled into it. "Angel—please be there . . ."

He heard a woman's voice reply—but it sounded way off in the distance and distorted, out of sync. And it was not Angel. He could tell.

But whoever it was . . . they were calling his name.

He started screaming back into the phone, "Who is this?" over and over, but it was as if the person couldn't hear him. They just kept calling out his name, echoing, from far away.

It went on for two agonizing minutes—and then suddenly, the sat phone went dead.

He hit the re-establish button, but all he got was a sound similar a busy signal—which he'd never heard on a 'Can before.

And then, there was nothing.

The message in the tiny display screen flashed: "No service."

Chapter Twelve

San Diego

Angel had just turned out her night light when she heard the buzzing.

She leapt from the bed and over to her bureau. Opening the bottom drawer she threw scads of frilly sleepwear all over the room until she found what she was looking for: her Tomato Can.

She answered it on the second buzz.

"Thank God!" was how she began. "I've been worried all day. Are you okay? I'm okay, but are you okay? Because if you're not, then I'm not."

Starr took a deep breath and tried not to cry. He'd been sitting at the top of the dune for nearly two hours, pressing the 'Can's activate button so many times over and over, he'd developed a blood blister on his right hand forefinger.

But on what had to be the 200th time, suddenly the "No Service" message disappeared from the sat-phone's tiny screen and he heard the clicks and clacks indicating the call was going through.

Why? Maybe a satellite had come over the horizon, or some kind of outer space interference had disappeared or maybe he was just really freaking lucky. But next thing he knew, he was talking to her.

The relief was indescribable.

"I'm okay," he told her, trying to maintain his cool. "Working on a bit of a problem—but first, did you call me on this earlier? Maybe two hours ago?"

"No way," she replied with emphasis. "After what we just went, through? I'm surprised you're using it to call me again."

"Well, it's only because we have a situation here," he told her.

He quickly explained what had happened, then spent the next several minutes trying to assure her that despite being shot down and crashing in the largest airplane ever built he was, really-really, okay.

However he *was* stranded in one of the most hostile places on Earth.

"The way this deal between Dima and the boys at Langley was set up, I'm not so sure anyone is going to be looking for us right away. We weren't flying a regular route. And I'm sure no one filed a flight plan or if they did it was fraudulent. And though I have a good idea, I'm not sure *exactly* where we are. That's why I need your help."

"Anything," she breathed.

He looked around again. To the east, a large storm was brewing. To his west, another huge weather system was coming in off the ocean. This is not good, he thought.

"Please Google a place called the Skeleton Coast," he asked. "Anything you can tell me about it will be a big help."

For the next two minutes, he heard a non-stop stream of information about this forbidding place.

It turned out The Skeleton Coast was well named because indeed there were skeletons everywhere. So many living things had been stranded and died here, the Namibian Government warned anyone entering the desert that after many years of lying around in such harsh conditions, all those bones break down into shards as sharp as razor blades. Many were hidden beneath the sands and could easily penetrate the sole of a boot.

Second unexpected fact: the place got so foggy, visibility could go down to nothing in just minutes, meaning you literally could not see your hand in front of you. It was so bad, insurance companies forbid ships from getting within 20 miles of the coastline.

Another government warning: The wreckage of ships dotting that coastline were hazardous to the touch because, the government saw fit to warn, they were all possibly "haunted by spirits." The same was true for any crashed aircraft.

So, razor-sharp bones, fog, ghosts . . .

Hundreds of species of creepy crawly things were found all over the desert too. Gigantic crickets, fire ants, spiders the size of a man's fist. Snakes that could eat anything, large herds of monster seals and king elephants at water's edge—with the entire area crawling with hyenas who see the seals, and other things, as easy pickings.

So, big bugs, dangerous predatory animals . . .

Then there was the wind. It was so violent sometimes, it could move tons of sand in a matter of minutes, meaning new skeletons were being uncovered all the time, as even uncovered ones were being lost to the eye again. No surprise it had blanketed the crash site so quickly.

And . . . when the wind conditions were very high, those ever-shifting sand dunes "sang." Caused, scientists believed, by billions of air particles caught between grains moving all at once. Starr had heard it shortly after climbing the grand dune. According to Angel, the sound had been compared to everything from thousands of voices singing the same note to the roar of a jet aircraft passing overhead.

One last footnote: parts of the Skeleton Coast were known as some of the best places in the world . . . to surf.

Angel ended her report by saying anxiously: "You've got to get out of there . . ."

"I agree," he replied, but then added: "But you know what that means, don't you?"

"I do," she answered. "But tell me anyway."

"It means, I'm going to have to make another call," he replied. "I'm going to have to call ONI headquarters—on the Tomato Can."

Again, possessing a Tomato Can was a security violation. Even though the Navy had phased them out, the case of Father Friendly and *his* Tomato Can was bizarre enough for Starr and Angel to vow never to use them unless absolutely necessary.

At the moment it was absolutely necessary.

"I will have to call them in DC," he went on. "And tell them what happened and where we are."

She hesitated for a moment, taking it in.

"But if you do that, they'll know we have the 'Cans and . . ." she let her voice trail off.

"And I might go to prison," he filled in the blank for her.

"I'll go instead," she told him, voice quivering. "I'll tell them I made you do it."

"That's never going to happen," he replied. "But let's face it, these Tomato Cans are more trouble than they are worth."

But she stopped him right there.

"Please don't ever say that," she said. "We've used them in times of real need, and times of real crisis, and we've helped each other out in ways that we could never have without them. And we are not doing anything detrimental to the country's security. In fact, most anytime we've used them it's to help *improve* that security—not compromise it. And I always feel that I can reach out and touch you no matter where you are or where I am. That's special to me."

Starr couldn't disagree. "It's special to me too," he relented. "But I still have to do it. There are people hurt here, people whose families might soon find out they're missing. I can't prevent someone searching for us for such a selfish reason as us not getting caught."

There was a brief silence, and then she said, "Of course, I couldn't sleep at night knowing we did anything differently."

The phone call was turning somber.

"Okay," he said. "I don't know when, but once they're on to us, they'll send someone out to you to take possession of your 'Can. That's why I wanted to talk to you first."

"I understand," she said, sadly.

"So, when that happens, here's what to do . . ." he began.

But before his next words could come out, he was greeted with an ear full of static.

And suddenly Angel was gone—their transmission abruptly terminated.

But then he heard the other voice.

A woman, calling him, from very far away.

Chilling . . .

He tried in vain to answer her, but she just kept calling his name, just as before.

Then that transmission completely went dead as well.

He desperately tried calling Angel back, but for the next hour got the dreaded window message again: "No service."

Finally he just dialed ONI headquarters in Suitland, Maryland. There was no sense putting it off any longer. He would give them the details of their crash—and essentially to turn himself in for misuse of classified Navy property, a serious criminal offense.

But once again, when he hit the activate button, the message screen flashed: "No service."

Chapter Thirteen

Starr remained at the top of the dune for the rest of the night, tending the fire and trying to make the sat phone work again.

He'd told Dima and Minky to get some rest, that he would take the first shift watching the flames and promised he'd wake them when it was their turn. But that never happened. Dima and Minky took his advice, went back to the survival egg, fell asleep and stayed that way. Just as he intended, Starr passed the dark hours up on the grand dune alone.

He fell into a bizarre routine. Throw something on the fire, take a swig of vodka, try to call Angel, fail, try to call ONI, fail, and then throw something else on the fire.

Sleep was out of the question; he was in a kind of trance. He couldn't take his eyes off the ocean, couldn't lose the notion that if he could only swim it, swim all the way back to the States, then hitch-hike across the country he could finally get home to Angel. He could probably do it in less than a week, with some luck. The first thing he would do: sit at her kitchen table and have an Irish beer with her.

This orgy of crushing self-regret had a soundtrack. Down below, in the near-pitch black sand bowl, the three Russian crewmen never stopped singing. Dozens of songs or just the same mournful song sung over and over—he didn't know. It all *sounded* the same, the Volga Boatmen in three-part harmony. It made him wonder more than once what would happen when the seemingly endless supply of vodka and sausages ran out and things got desperate. Hungover, hopeless and hungry—it could get ugly.

Mixed into this all-night serenade were some stunning desert sounds. The wind blowing sand all around him. The massive waves crashing against the forbidding coastline a half mile away. Various desert bugs, tweeting and clicking and an endless stream of nocturnal bird calls. And sometimes, the horrifying cries of something getting eaten by something else.

It seemed to go on forever, but the sun finally came up over his shoulder, lighting up that vast ocean and killing his dream forever of taking a long swim home.

He finally descended the mount, so dejected he hardly noticed his hangover.

Stumbling into the survival egg, he found Dima curled up in the far corner, still asleep, a piece of foam rubber as his pillow. Minky was awake though. She was sitting beside Misha, also asleep and being cooled by what looked like a common household fan.

It was from the remains of the airplane's huge flight deck, one of the big, noisy fans that did almost nothing to dampen the sweltering heat inside the An-225B. But now, here it was, running and keeping the injured Misha cool—or at least cooler.

"How?" was all Starr could wearily ask Minky.

She pointed to a small battery next to Misha's bed. It was attached to a cigarette-pack sized device Starr recognized as an actuator. Basically little motors, they were a key component in any new high-performance car—as well as billions of other machines around the world, including airplanes. This one had two wires running from its back into the bottom of the fan, everything held in place by lots of duct tape.

Battery to actuator to moving fan. It was crude but ingenious.

"Boris?" Starr asked Minky.

She nodded and said: "He's out back . . ."

Starr walked into the tent and only then did he realize something: the Russian crewmen were singing as they worked. That's what they'd been doing all this time—and that's what they were doing now. They were singing and drinking, but also working. Their project: putting Dima's sailplane back together.

Starr couldn't believe it really. When he'd seen the sailplane before, it was just one pile of junk amongst a lot of piles of junk they'd collected under the tent.

Never did he think they intended to put it back together.

It was a Merlin-122X sailplane.

As designed, it had long, strappy wings, 60 feet end to end, giving it the appearance of a mini-U2 spy plane. The fuselage was half as long, tapered and slender, with a high, flat wing for a tail. Ninety percent of the aircraft was made from molded pearl-white polymer fibers; its canopy had a distinctive bubble-top look. It also carried a ballistic parachute. In case of trouble, it would deploy from the top of the sailplane's mid-fuselage and gently lower the aircraft to the ground.

But again, this Merlin had not survived the crash intact. Once the Russian crewmen salvaged as much as they could find and reassembled it, they discovered while the fuselage forward of the wings was dinged and cracked, it was more or less intact. But everything from the wings back had been shredded into dozens of pieces. Plus, all the plane's control wires had snapped and were gone, the cockpit glass seemed shattered beyond any repair and the tiny, skid-like landing gear was crushed and useless.

This particular sailplane had never flown before. It was actually a work still in progress when it left Russia. Once settled in the USA, Dima had planned to add a small jet engine to the plane, making it a powered glider, which were now all the rage.

That tiny jet engine was sitting on a work bench at the Lockheed test facility in Burbank. But the mounting plate and reinforcing collar needed for it to be fitted onto the sailplane's upper fuselage had already been installed.

Starr was amazed how much work the Russian crewmen had done on the plane since he last saw it. Laid out in sections under the tent, Stan and Oleg were in the process of wrapping its rear quarter with long pieces of the ubiquitous yellow caution tape, melting it slightly and then adding more layers until it was somewhat sturdy. It looked haphazard but so far it was doing a good job at keeping the rear half of the fuselage and the tail wing together.

Meanwhile, Boris was working around the area just behind the cracked bubble canopy, where the intended mini jet was to be installed. He'd taken a battery pack from the electric Rolls and assembled an army of actuators around it, creating something the size of a lawn mower engine. He'd then placed it inside the mini-jet's empty engine mounting, once again using miles of duct tape to keep everything intact.

Re-purposed guitar strings replaced the control wires, and the rear half of the broken bubble canopy had been removed, leaving the front portion as a workable, if jagged windscreen. A dozen or so basketballs had been attached under the long wing, reason unknown.

Boris saw Starr had joined them. With one word, he told his comrades to stop singing. Then he flipped a crudely wired switch duct-taped to the right wing. Suddenly things were turning, fan motors were whirring and the long wing's rudimentary flaps were going up and down. For want of a better word, they'd electrified the thing.

Starr was amazed. Minky was suddenly beside him, attracted by the noise. She nodded towards Boris.

"He is a very determined man," she said. "They all are . . ."

Starr asked her to ask him how he thought it would work.

Boris replied with a long stream of Russian. Minky translated: "He says, 'We carry it to top of highest dune. Start engine, push it over the side. Air gets under wings. It lifts off and we go. We go look for help.'"

"And what's with the basketballs?" Starr wanted to know.

Minky asked the question and Boris answered in two words: *Deshevo chassy.*

Cheap landing-gear . . .

Starr took it all in. The three singing, drinking crewmen had indeed rebuilt the sailplane into something that looked like it might actually . . . fly.

Still he couldn't believe he was going to ask the next question.

"What does it need to be complete?"

Boris didn't require a translation this time. He was immediately crest-fallen, falling to the seat of his pants. He replied himself, saying in very pained, very weary Russian: *Nuzhen propellarinski* . . .

We need a propeller . . .

Chapter Fourteen

It turned out Starr arrived just as the sail plane re-building project had hit a brick wall.

The three men had done all they could, with what they had. But they still needed a *propellarinski* . . .

And not just any *propellarinski* . . .

It had to be shaped just right, have the right contours, be strong enough to take a lot of revolutions yet not be too heavy for its own good.

Through Minky, Boris explained they'd tried many things, from stray pieces of metal to cracked turbine blades, to simple pieces of wood carved out of the dashboard of Dima's demolished Rolls. Nothing worked.

The gloom of revealing this cold truth suddenly enveloped them. So close, yet so far.

All work halted on the plane soon after that, the inevitable exhaustion kicking in. A sandstorm was blowing up and it was quickly clear it would be much larger than anything they'd experienced since getting here. So they secured the still-born DIY aircraft as best they could and then retreated to the survival egg.

The shelter was carpeted in foam rubber now, so it was a little less uncomfortable. Stan had drilled some vent holes on the roof which relieved the stuffiness and they'd retrieved an astounding number of sausages and intact vodka bottles. So they ate and drank vodka throughout the late morning and into the afternoon, taking turns comforting Misha. Outside the sandstorm raged on unabated, killing any chances of rebuilding the bonfire anytime soon.

By the time the sun began to set, everyone was asleep or passed out—except Starr.

He took the time to try the Tomato Can again—once for Angel, once for ONI HQ. But in addition to getting the same soul-crushing message of "No Service," the light inside the sat-phone's tiny read-out screen was growing dimmer. His battery was running out.

Just what he needed.

Really facing the abyss now, Starr just lay back on a charred piece of foam and finally fell asleep too.

A few hours went by.

He dreamed fitfully. About Angel, about the Tomato Cans, about the raging sea and a mountain top buried in snow. At one point, he saw a jet aircraft passing low over his head. Engines roaring, it was very loud and was trying to drop a bomb on him.

It was so real, he willed himself awake. It took a few seconds, but then his eyes opened and he realized where he was.

But he still heard the sound of a jet engine, passing overhead.

They all did.

Everyone was suddenly awake and excited that this might be a rescue aircraft. Minky became especially animated. She yanked open the egg's doors and started waving her arms skyward.

"My God!" she screamed. "We are down here!"

But the violent sandstorm was still raging, and she was gone a second later, sucked right out of the egg and into the night.

Starr leapt for the opening just in time to see her disappear into the thickest fog imaginable, made truly fantastic by the heavy swirling winds. Fog was more usual in places with no wind. Not here, though, not now. It looked like a blizzard of steam, blowing around at high speed; a horror movie's special effects come to life.

There came a sudden shift in direction and suddenly the wind was trying to suck them *all* out of the Egg. They had to hold on tight to something to prevent suffering Minky's fate. And above it all, that same strange noise—a jet engine, roaring right above their heads and all around them. It never went away.

With help from Oleg and Stan, Starr forced the doors closed. It sealed them off from much of the noise and tumult outside.

"Wait—we can't leave her out there!" Dima screamed.

But Starr was already on the case. He zipped up his NILE windbreaker and pulled his baseball cap down as far as it would go. He retrieved his Glock 9mm from his ankle holster, checked that it was loaded, and then took their small but powerful flashlight.

"Everyone stays put here," he told them. "No one leaves until I get back . . ."

Then he slipped out into the storm.

Chapter Fifteen

It was like walking into a tornado.

The wind was literally blowing in all directions and it immediately took hold of Starr and tried to carry him away, like it had Minky.

He had to stand firm, though, freeze in place, fight the gale and get his bearings. It was a real struggle, as he wondered whether this was a good idea or not. But while this was happening, above everything else, he still heard what seemed so much like the roar of a jet engine.

But it was not.

He realized the strange sound wasn't even mechanical.

It was coming from the dunes. They were singing, just like Angel told him they would. But this time, the wind was moving so quickly through the loose sand that the combined effect sounded not like a choir but like a jet engine—one that was in trouble, losing its ferocity for a few seconds before regaining its full throat.

It quickly devolved into a completely bizarre situation. The wind blowing the thick fog. The dunes roaring. There were even flashes of lightning. And Starr could also hear something else: the sound of hyenas yipping nearby.

But above it all, he also heard Minky's voice, calling out for help.

He began to trudge slowly in her direction, but the wind and the sand bowl played tricks with sound. Trying hard not to trip over anything in the thick fog, the powerful little flashlight not doing much good in the blowing murk, he spent the next ten minutes essentially walking blind, fighting to put one foot in front of the other, calling out as loud as he could: "Where are you?"

Ten minutes turned into twenty. He went up and over at least a dozen sand dunes, though not as high as the ones bracketing the Sand Bowl. Minky's voice, still crying out, sometimes seemed right in front of him. But it moved as he moved, and with every step, she sounded like she was getting farther and farther away.

Suddenly he could hear waves crashing—but this sound too was distorted, loud but then retreating. He was still essentially moving blind; for all he knew, the waves could be breaking right in front of him, ready to sweep him away. He might be taking that swim in the ocean just yet.

So he stopped walking—and the only thing he could hear for a moment was his heart beating out of his chest.

But then, Minky cried out again and this time it sounded close by and coming from only one direction. He immediately tried to key in on her location, moving very slowly. After a few seconds, he directed the flashlight down to his feet and saw he was walking in very shallow water. A blast of salt air hit him broadside and in the next moment, a huge wave came crashing down on top of him, knocking him down and nearly dragging him out to sea.

It was only that his short term ESP gave him a half second warning that he'd braced himself at the last possible instant. Still, it seemed like he'd been hit by a ton of bricks. It took him three tries to get to his feet, thrashing around in the dark, the water over his head. Finally, he fought against the tide and made it to shore— but just barely.

When he was able to stand again, he directed the flashlight beam a few feet in front of him and saw a most ghastly sight.

There was a gigantic seal not ten feet in front of him, on its back and torn open, blood and guts everywhere. Surrounding the creature was a pack of hyenas.

There was an old shipwreck behind them. Hanging for dear life to its rusted bow section was Minky.

The hyenas all turned towards him; there were six of them. No yipping, no laughing. Just a barely audible growl. Each one went into an attack position, lowering its head and baring teeth. Their eyes seemed to glow.

Starr had a strange thought at that moment. Did they see him as a competitor for the seal or just another meal?

Either way, the pack momentarily forgot about the seal and started moving in Starr's direction. Flashlight blazing, he retreated two steps, aware that he might get hit by another massive wave and that would end the whole thing right then and there.

But this did not happen, so he backed up a few more feet. The pack followed, moving away from the shipwreck and Minky.

Two more feet and the pack was now directly in front of him. They began yipping and yapping at this point, obviously getting agitated, and moving to surround him.

He waited—and it seemed like forever—for the lead creature to make the first leap for him, to try to nip him or grab the sleeve of his jacket. That's when he raised his other hand, and blasted off three shots from his Glock.

The hyena was hit in mid-air by the fusillade. Knocked backwards, he went head over heels into the water. The rest of the hyenas immediately fell back on themselves and began running away at full speed, yipping quite loudly now, their frightened howls fading into the fog and night.

Starr ran back to the shipwreck and helped Minky down. She collapsed in his arms, astounded that she was still alive and that it was Starr who saved her.

"A Russian man would never do that for me," she told him in fractured English. She hugged him tightly.

But now they had another problem. They were totally lost.

It would be dangerous to try to make their way through the storm and the fog and the hyenas back to the crash site. He spotted a tall outcrop of rock hanging over the beach. Strangely it looked like the palm of a huge, uplifted hand. It would provide shelter from the wind, the sand and maybe hungry wild animals.

This is where they went. Starr helped Minky climb up into it and they huddled and tried to get warm.

It seemed to take hours, but from here, they watched the last of the surreal storm finally blow over them, its tail end battering its way across the desert and at last, out to sea.

Chapter Sixteen

Starr was dreaming about a gigantic peanut, still in its shell, hovering above him, when he finally woke up.

It was early morning; a sea haze had settled on the shoreline. Minky was entwined around him, almost intimately, her flight uniform now in tatters in some very out of the way places.

They were still atop the hand-shaped outcrop looking down on the breaking waves. But they were no longer alone.

Trying to shield the sun and sand from his eyes, Starr realized an elephant was standing right next to where they lay.

It looked like a monster. A mammoth with a buzz cut, it towered over them, its trunk sized more like a tree trunk, moving in slow motion.

And it was looking right at him. Two baseball-sized brown eyes, staring into his soul, as if asking: Where's *my* peanut?

He gently shook Minky awake. She came to in a start, looked at the huge creature no more than ten feet away, and cried: "Not again!"

This caused the animal to shift just enough for Starr to see a person was riding atop it. A young boy with dark orange skin was also looking down at them. He didn't appear mystified or particularly curious about why they were there. He seemed very calm, as if he'd been waiting some time for them to wake.

Minky held onto Starr even tighter.

"Do you still have your pistol?" she whispered to him.

The boy studied them, making sure they were both awake. Then he made a hand gesture, fingers together, but with thumb extended, starting at the top of his head and then dropping as if to the ground. It looked like an airplane crashing.

Starr nodded enthusiastically. He was sure the boy meant their crash site—and after all the excitement last night, he had no idea where they were or how best to get back. Maybe boy and beast could show them the way.

The boy indicated they should follow him. He turned the elephant around and they started off. Starr and Minky climbed out of the rock, back to the ever shifting sands of the desert below and fell in behind the huge creature. The boy never looked back down at them, never really acknowledged they were in tow. And he had the elephant going at a fairly quick pace; at times, Starr and Minky had to jog in order to keep up.

After going up and over several unfamiliar looking dunes, they came to another huge sand bowl, but this one was much closer to the sea. That's when Starr realized the kid was not leading them back to the An-225B site. Instead he was taking them to a small oasis in the middle of this bowl.

Only on arrival was it clear what the kid was trying to tell them with his hand gesture earlier.

Caught in the trees and wrapped in miles of its own wires, was a wrecked and rusting helicopter. It was an old Bell 206 Jet Ranger model, popular in the 1960s and it looked like it had been here just about that long. The two crew members—now skeletons—were still strapped to the seats. And indeed some of their bones had edges as sharp as razor blades.

This was the crash the kid meant.

But why bring them here?

The kid pointed down from his elephant, not at the helicopter itself but at its tail rotor section. Hanging half way off but looking none the worse for the wear was the copter's tail rotor.

It hit Starr and Minky at the same time.

"Oh my God," she gasped. "It's a *propellinski* . . ."

Chapter Seventeen

What happened next would be by far the strangest thing Starr had experienced since crashing in the middle of nowhere and maybe in his life so far.

He examined the rotor blade. It was in remarkably good shape; even better the bolts that connected it to the rest of the tail section had conveniently rusted away, allowing him to pull the blade off with ease.

He knew it was way too big to be fitted on the Merlin sailplane. But maybe Boris could cut off the ends somehow and shorten it. If that happened, who knows where it would lead?

Minky too had been engrossed in studying the rotor blade. She'd peppered him with questions throughout. Will it work? Can it work? He stayed optimistic when answering her, saying that it was the closest thing they had to a real propeller and they both knew how determined a man Boris was.

They did all this is less than a minute. But when they looked up again, they suddenly realized two things: Another extremely thick Skeleton Coast fog had rolled in on them. And the boy and the elephant were gone.

They were both shaken by these two events. They had been here long enough to know that these fogs were the real killers in this hellish place. If you managed to survive the plane crash or the shipwreck, getting lost in one of these silent storms would mostly likely be the end of you. You were easy prey for the razor sharp bones, the poisonous bugs or the hyenas. And if they didn't get you, starvation or the ghosts would.

"Where did he go?" Minky asked, trying hard to keep her cool. "We need him to rescue us. Or at least get us back to everyone else . . ."

Starr looked in every direction, but by now he could barely see an arm's length away. The sand around the oasis was too loose to leave any footprints, so there was no way they could follow the creature's trail. It was so odd, their suddenly being alone, that it almost seemed like they'd imagined the whole thing.

In fact, Minky even said to him: "Did we just dream all this?'

Starr tried to call on his little bit of psychic ability to help them out here, at the same time knowing it just didn't work that way.

They had to get back to the ocean; at least there they knew where they were and maybe if they found the rock outcrop again and then maybe the body of the seal they might somehow find their way back to the An-225B crash site.

Maybe, maybe, maybe . . .

He figured they had walked for about ten minutes to the oasis, so that meant the outcrop and the ocean should be about a quarter mile away. But in which direction? They tried, but they couldn't even hear the waves.

They had to get to higher ground, but Starr knew it could prove fatal if they split up. Plus, leaving the oasis with no firm plan or direction would be foolish.

A possible solution popped into his head.

They started unraveling some of the wires twisted around the copter wreck. In a few minutes they had at least five hundred feet of it. Starr tied one end around the largest and strongest palm tree then wrapped the other end around his waist. Then he gave Minky his Glock and said: "Stay here. I'll try to find the nearest dune, climb it and maybe I'll hear something or see something."

She agreed right away, grabbing the gun and the rotor and sitting down next to the big tree. She put her hand on the wire.

"But if I pull on this hard," she said, "you have to come back to me. Okay?"

"*Konieczno,*" he replied. "Of course . . ."

And this was when it really got weird.

Starr set out, unraveling his roll of wire as he trudged along in the thick fog.

He kept his eyes on his feet. He could just barely see them, but he wanted to be careful that he didn't step on some razor bones or awaken some gigantic monstrous, poisonous spider. He also wanted to know when he reached a sand dune.

After about a minute of walking, he found what he was looking for—the bottom of a dune. Up he went, unfurling the wire with every careful step. He seemed to be climbing forever, and was worried his life line was going to run out, when suddenly he found himself close to the top of one of the desert's giant dunes.

He got to the end of the wire just as he reached the summit. He immediately concentrated on listening for the waves, realizing it might be the difference between life and death should he hear them or not.

At first he heard nothing. It was still foggy up here, and almost as dark as twilight. But he could at least make out the tops of other dunes nearby. Even if he couldn't hear the waves crashing, maybe he could see the ocean?

He faced what he thought was west, but then something caught his eye. It wasn't in front of him, but off to the right, atop the next dune over, maybe 300 feet away.

There was someone over there. He could just barely make out the figure in the deep morning mist. It wasn't the kid; this was an adult. And they seemed to be point-ing to something even farther to their right.

At that moment, the wind started up and the sand be-gan singing again and this time it did indeed sound like a choir of thousands of voices, lifted in one note. The wind also blew away more of the fog along the tops of the dunes and a moment later, Starr was able to see the figure clearly.

His next breath caught in his throat. This person was dressed in a full length dark robe with a large hood covering their head and hiding their face in shadow.

His first thought was . . .Oh my God, the Grim Reap-er really exists?

But in the next second, he realized this was not so.

What he was looking at on the top of the next dune over was a monk. Hood, cassock, rope belt. The works.

He was standing almost perfectly still, still pointing off to his right, but looking directly over at Starr.

Starr froze in place for what seemed like a very long time, trying to make some sense out of what he was seeing.

A monk?

Out here?

He closed his eyes, wondering what he would see when he opened them again. The sand was still singing and the wind was still blowing, but in that moment, eyes still closed, he thought he heard something else, some-thing that seemed to be reverberating inside his head, bouncing between his ear drums.

The mysterious woman's voice on the other end of the Tomato Can. Calling his name, endlessly. The sat-phone was back at the survival egg, hidden in his stuff, turned off to preserve the battery's life. But at that moment it was like he was holding it up to his ear, the volume turned up to 11.

That voice . . .

Calling him . . .

When he opened his eyes again, the figure on top of the next dune was gone.

Starr reeled himself back down the dune and was running by the time he reached the oasis.

Minky had the Glock ready but was hugely relieved when she saw him. She jumped up and embraced him, long and tight.

"You are brave," she whispered in his ear. "Thank you for being so brave."

"We have to go," he told her. "Right now . . ."

He gathered up the rotor; she kept the Glock.

But he kept the wire tied around the tree. He was no whiz-kid at math, but he knew something about turning an angle.

He knew where he was when he'd reached the end of his tether atop the dune. Back at the starting point he knew if they walked in the opposite direction and reached the end of the wire, all they would need to do, is keep moving to their left and eventually they would reach the top of the dune where he'd seen the mysterious figure. Or so he hoped.

"You have a plan?" she asked him excitedly. "Do you know something?"

He couldn't find the words to explain it to her; he couldn't explain it to himself.

"I know this will sound crazy," he finally replied. "But I think there might be a monastery around here someplace."

They followed the wire to its end and started walking to the left and were soon climbing another dune.

The higher they went, the more Starr realized his high school math had paid off. They soon found themselves at the top of the dune where he'd seen the monk.

And on the other side, where he'd seen the monk pointing and bizarrely free of any of the thick mist, was home—the An-225B crash site.

It had been just over that next dune all along.

Chapter Eighteen

It took Boris less than an hour to break the ends off the tail rotor and attach it to the Merlin 122X sailplane.

Again, a lot of hammering and a mile or so of duct tape was needed, but indeed Boris was a determined man. When he gave his electric motor a quick try out, the damn thing worked. For the thirty seconds he had it on, the *propellinski* stayed attached.

That was all Boris really wanted to know. Stating they had no time to waste, he declared the plane was ready to launch.

But, even though they worked in teams—Starr, Minky and Dima, then Stan, Oleg and Boris—it still took another hour to get the sailplane up to the top of the grand dune. Carrying it would not be the correct term. Dragging, pulling and pushing were more accurate, with a lot of swearing and lost ground in between. One team would get the awkward airframe up ten feet, but then it would slide back half that distance or more. The second team would then take over, but usually with similar results.

It was two steps forward, one back, the entire way up. By the time they reached the top, they were all beyond exhausted, the broiling sun having beaten down on them mercilessly the whole time. It was only after a brief rest that they started thinking about the launch in earnest.

There was never any question who was going to be the pilot. Starr had several hundred hours in the air in various airframes and Dima too was an accomplished flier. But Boris never put it out to a vote or asked for anyone's opinion.

He'd been the brains behind this operation; he would be the one behind the controls.

His plan was to use the electric motor to fly the sailplane as high as he could, as fast as he could. Once he had some air under his wings, he would do a quick recon from that height, hope to spot some kind of civilization and then head in that direction.

Oddly it was a plan Starr could get behind or at least understand its madness.

This wasn't the movies and the *propellinski* wasn't a real propeller. It would be a miracle if it remained attached for more than a few seconds in flight.

But because the aircraft was a glider, it might get high enough to find an air current and then fly on its own.

Boris had even devised a way for them to launch the sailplane. Using hook-like fasteners he'd found in the debris of one of the An-225B's engines, he'd attached them to the rear of the wing, five pairs in all.

The idea was for the others to use the handles to hold the plane in place while he started the engine and ran it up to full speed. They were, in effect, acting as human brakes.

At the moment the engine had built up enough power, they would let go and sort of slingshot him up into the great beyond.

And that's what happened.

Boris climbed in, turned everything on, started his electric motor going, and gradually increased the RPMs until it was hard for the others to hold the plane back any longer.

"*Otpusty!*" Boris cried. "Let go!"

They did and off he went, into the wind, heading west, towards the sea.

But not five seconds into the flight, Boris pulled all the way back on the controls and suddenly he was going straight up, using the momentum gained by the take off to get some altitude under him.

It was a ballsy move and not one they'd expected.

And he succeeded. . . for about another ten seconds.

It was when he'd reached a height of about 1,000 feet that things started to go wrong.

As it turned out, it was not the make-shift engine that doomed the flight—it was the tail section. The yellow caution tape mummifying process only held together for so long before it began to unravel.

Boris climbed about another 200 feet or so, but that's when the tail came off. The sailplane, or what was left of it, did a 180 and started coming down just as fast as it had gone up.

They all watched in horror—all except Starr. Thanks to a burst of his short-term ESP, he knew what would happen next.

He found himself whispering: "Three . . . two . . . one . . ."

At that moment, a small burst of flame emitted from the plummeting sail plane—and then a huge very pink parachute deployed from right behind the cockpit.

It filled with air just in time to slow down the broken plane and carry its very determined pilot to a rough but successful landing on the beach about a half mile away.

Chapter Nineteen

Starr, Stan and Oleg ran over the dunes and down to the beach.

They found Boris sitting in the shallow water, looking more sullen and dejected than usual. He was allowing the waves to batter him from the back.

They helped him to dry land. Except for a few cuts and scrapes, he seemed unhurt. The Merlin sailplane was close by in about three feet of water, also being battered by the waves. The front half was cracked and dented but still intact. The wrapped tail section was hanging by a single strand of yellow caution tape. The only reason the aircraft hadn't sank was because the basketballs attached under its wing were keeping it afloat.

They pulled it up onto the beach and assessed the damage. It had been a valiant effort just getting the thing airborne, but clearly it would be its one and only flight.

Stan could speak a little English. Starr asked him to tell Boris that they all appreciated what he'd done and that it was too bad his bravery wasn't rewarded. But Boris dismissed Starr's message with the wave of his hand. He reeled off twenty seconds of rapid-fire Russian, which Stan translated.

"He says his mission was not a failure," Stan explained.

Starr was surprised. "How so?"

Stan just shrugged. "He says when he was at the top of his flight, he could see about fifty miles down the coastline."

"And?"

"And he said he saw people down there . . . surfing."

"Surfing?" Starr repeated back to him. "Really?"

"That's what he said," Stan insisted.

But suddenly, Starr could not hear him. He heard a familiar buzzing in his head instead. His short-term ESP was kicking in.

That's when he indicated that they all should just . . . listen.

And they did—and soon enough they all heard it. A deep roar, haunting, disturbing, still way off but getting closer. It was not the singing dunes this time, not the crashing waves or not the blustering wind.

This was something else.

Airplane engines. Real ones. Coming their way.

Rescue planes?

Had Angel made the call to ONI anyway?

The answer to both questions was no.

These were jet fighters, Starr could tell almost right away.

216

And they were not here to rescue them.

Just the opposite.

They all looked to the east, shielding their eyes from brutal hot sun and saw two specks coming in their direction.

It was the pair of Su-34s. The ones that'd shot them down.

No one needed to be told to take cover. Stan and Starr hastily dragged the sailplane out of the water and put it under the cover of some sea bushes nearby. Oleg and Boris retrieved the bright pink parachute, quickly folded it and stuck it in the sand.

Then they took up positions under an outcrop of rock, hidden but still able to watch the sky.

The Russian-built warplanes went over a few seconds later. They were loud, but they weren't heading towards the wreckage site, but out over the water.

"They're not looking for us here," Starr said to his companions. "They're looking for wreckage at sea."

The warplanes did several orbits about a half mile offshore, before finally banking northward and leaving the area quickly.

"We've got to get out of here," Starr said once they were gone. "If they were here looking for wreckage at sea and didn't find any, then they'll be back and they'll start looking over dry land next."

"But *how* do we get out?" Stan replied. "Flying is no longer possible."

Starr looked at what was left of Boris's contraption, stuck up under the sea bushes.

"That thing isn't ever going to fly again," he agreed. But he thought for another long moment, studying the odd, Rube Goldberg machine in a different light, then added: "It might float, though . . ."

Chapter Twenty

They knew their way back to the crash site from here.

It was a matter of walking east, in an almost straight line from the beach, weaving in and out of a few large dunes until they could see the largest one of all, the grand dune, the place where they'd launched the sailplane.

Dima and Minky were waiting for them. Starr immediately asked for a group meeting—including Misha, who this impacted too.

Once inside the survival egg, the survivors gathered around Misha's bed and told Starr he had the floor.

"Those fighter planes will be back," he began. "Someone wants confirmation that we crashed and as they didn't spot any wreckage out to sea, they'll start working inward. They have look-down radar, terrain-following gear, infra-red scopes. I'm no expert but those things might be able to pick out a crash site in amongst the sand. Plus there are a few fires still smoldering out there.

"That's why we have to get out of here now—and I mean all of us."

"But, how?" Boris wanted to know, with Minky translating. "We swim fifty miles down the coast and hook up with the surfer dudes?"

"No, not swim," Starr replied. "But I think we can sail there, on what's left of the Merlin."

"But it is airplane," Boris said. "Not sailboat."

"I think it can be something else," Starr told him. "I think you can turn it in a powerboat. And I think you can get us fifty miles down the coastline."

While Boris obviously enjoyed the praise, it still took a long time to persuade him of this idea. His main objection: He was convinced he could get the Merlin to fly again.

He insisted, "If we all believe, it will happen. But we must all believe."

It took several interventions by Minky and by Dima himself to convince Boris that they didn't have the time to rebuild the Merlin as an airplane before the Su-34s came back and finished the job.

Turn the elevators into small rudders, they told him and have the actuators still work them. Use the rotor blade not as an air propeller but something more like on a swamp boat. Angled a different way, it could propel them along the surface of the ocean.

And Boris could still be the pilot—and captain of the ship.

While the engineer couldn't argue the contraption would probably float, due to the basketballs attached to its underbelly, it took one last private chat with Dima to turn him around. At that moment, Starr was convinced the billionaire offered the engineer a monetary incentive to overcome his stubbornness.

However it happened, Boris finally agreed.

Chapter Twenty-One

It was easier for them to move Boris's tools down the beach than to haul the Merlin back up to the crash site.

Stan and Oleg helped him carry the essential gear to the shoreline. Meanwhile Starr, Dima and Minky devised the least painful way to move Misha. They first built a large stretcher of foam rubber, netting and wooden rails from the wreck of the Rolls. Before placing her on this litter, they wrapped the top half of her body in more foam rubber, tied by, what else, yellow caution tape, stabilizing her two broken arms as best they could.

Then she drank about a half liter of vodka and said: "*poyekhali!*"

Let's go . . .

Time was their biggest enemy now.

Starr had done the math: if the Su-34s came from the nearest Russian-friendly country that would be Angola. If they returned to their last base to refuel, then a turn-around trip like that could be done in less than two hours.

This meant they could be back in the area within the hour. If that happened, and if the survivors were caught out in the open on the beach, with the firepower the Su-

34s could carry, this long unpleasant ball game would finally be over.

But once again, in the speediest of fashion, Boris did the adjustments required to turn the sailplane into a boat. Within an hour of getting his tools, he'd converted the ailerons into rudders and, by re-attaching the electric motor about ten inches off the top of the fuselage, turned the propeller into a large fan.

More basketballs were attached under the wing and along its sides, increasing the buoyancy. The hand grips they'd used for the first air launch were now on the leading edge of the wing, so the passengers, lying flat out, could hang on to them. Safety harnesses found in the wreck were also attached, allowing each passenger to get tied in as well.

But they still had more hurdles to get over.

One more forbidding aspect of the Skeleton Coast was its tides were extremely unpredictable. Not the timing, but the height and ferocity. Each incoming wave could vary wildly from a minor white cap to a monster that could make some Maui-wowie waves look tiny.

Then there were times when surface conditions could be as mild as a lake, where there'd hardly be any waves at all. But that could change rapidly as well. For Starr's plan to work, it would almost have to be a very calm situation.

So while Boris toiled away on the Marlin, Starr kept his eye on the waves. With each one to hit the shore he wanted to tell himself they were getting smaller and some of them definitely were. By the time Boris declared he was done, Starr had sensed a pattern. Five minutes of really big waves, followed by a few more minutes of semi-scary ones, followed by about three minutes of calm before the big boys started coming in again.

When they dragged the Merlin back down to the shore, the waves weren't tsunami-strength but they were two or three feet high, enough to make everything in their scheme that more difficult. If the pattern held, though, the waves would calm down for a few minutes very shortly.

But Boris being Boris, it wasn't going to be simply let's put the Marlin back in the ocean and go. He insisted on testing the contraption first, by himself, which he did, against some semi-scary waves. The man was without fear. As the others watched from the shore, filled with anticipation, Boris climbed into the plane's cockpit, picked up two hands full of guitar-string control wires, started the fan engine and pushed the throttle to the max. It took a moment for everything to catch, but a moment after they did, off he went. Suddenly he was zipping along the tops of those waves, sometimes nearly going airborne, controlling the make-shift air boat by pulling back and forth on the control wires wrapped around his hands. Back and forth he went, battling the spray and growing waves, but actually moving along at a rapid clip.

Those on shore couldn't believe it.

The damn thing actually worked.

All this took another half hour and by now, the sun was beginning to dip and the Su-34s could be just minutes away.

This time they really did have to go. And quickly.

They began the process of getting themselves secured to the floating sailplane. They first lowered the foam-wrapped Misha into the pilot's seat and made sure she was packed in tight. They'd found a single life preserver in the An-225B's wreckage and put it around her as well.

Then Starr helped strap in Minky on the wing to the left of the cockpit, so she was next to Misha. Then came Starr's place.

On the other side of the wing, Stan, Oleg and Dima were also tightening themselves in.

But suddenly something they'd all missed became abundantly clear. There was no place for Boris. No place for him to tie in or hang on to like the others. What's more, in the test trials he'd been inside the cockpit, where the crude controls were. How could he control the contraption if Misha was in the pilot's seat?

They all looked at each other and thought the same thing: how could we have fucked this up?

But when Starr pointed out the problem to the engineer, Boris replied: "I am the captain. I will hold on where I can."

There was no time to argue. Boris took up station right behind the cockpit, lying flat out on the remains of the rear fuselage, with the two combines of guitar-strings in his hands. But with the propeller fan spinning just inches above his head and nothing to grab on to, it was a tenuous position at best.

Boris checked that all his passengers were properly secured then started the power pack. The conglomeration of one big electrical motor working with a handful of actuators and moving fan belts made for a whipping sound, nothing like a more typical aircraft engine.

But it was powerful. Just as soon as Boris pulled the switch which engaged the old helicopter's tail rotor, the Merlin began moving very rapidly out into the deeper water.

The anxious passengers held on tight, Starr being no different. Within a minute they were really tooling along, but right away Boris was nearly overwhelmed trying to keep the strange craft steady and heading in one direction: south, where he'd seen the surfers during his brief recon flight.

They were soon nearly a quarter mile offshore, the coastline getting smaller with every second. The converted Merlin was roaring along the top of the water at such a speed, there were times that they actually went airborne and stayed there for longer than gravity should have allowed. They'd always come back down with a great splash, but again with considerable skill, Boris was able to make the crash landings actually manageable if not bone-crushing.

The whole thing was so crazy everyone, including Misha, began laughing hysterically—as if they were on some kind of outrageous amusement park ride. Scared but excited.

At one point, Boris yelled over to Starr: "We might fly yet!"

"It will be a shorter journey then!" he yelled back.

Starr couldn't believe he was even having this conversation, but as it turned out, it would be an interrupted talk, as two really bad things happened next.

Starr had a slight advance warning of the first one. It just hit him quickly enough for him to yell to the others, and especially Boris: "Stay down!"

A moment later the two Su-34s went over their heads at about Mach 1.

Starr was sure the fighters were moving too fast to spot them, but they were also so low, their engine wash swamped the little machine, turning it upside down.

That's when the second bad thing happened.

A trio of typically gigantic Skeleton Coast waves arrived at the same moment, slamming into the upturned vessel and tossing it in the air. The first wave caused the fan engine to become disconnected from its mounts; the second wave washed it away completely.

But the third wave was so powerful, in a bit of perverse luck, it flipped the engine-less sailplane upright again—with everyone still strapped in place.

Starr gasped for breath, astonished they were right-side up again. Even better, the Su-34s were gone.

But so was Boris.

Chapter Twenty-Two

They drifted for hours, at times certain they were going to be swept too far out to sea, other times fearing they would be dashed up against the killer rocks. But still the currents kept them heading south.

They called out for Boris throughout the night and looked for him as hard as they could, even though they knew the conditions were not working in his favor. They never gave up, though, each person taking turns shouting his name and then they'd all wait, hoping for a reply. But one never came.

It was morning when they were spotted—not by any rescue party or enemy, but by a group of South African surfers. They were a bunch of real hang-five dudes and were beside themselves with both amazement and amusement when they saw the floating wing approaching them. By this point the contraption was falling apart and they were sure it had somehow fallen out of the sky.

The surfers helped the girls off and onto the surfboards and paddled them into shore. Then a few more were able to push the broken sailplane in far enough that it eventually washed onto the beach.

On reaching dry land again, Starr was glad to see that they had indeed reached civilization. The beach was in front of a high-class resort, lined with cabanas and lounges, with waiters hurrying about, delivering food and drink.

The floating wing's arrival became an immediate center of curiosity. A large crowd gathered around it. The survivors had previously vowed to say very little to anybody about their adventure, though. At this point, the less talk the better.

While the resort's lifeguards were tending to his fellow travelers at the water's edge, Starr was distracted by a familiar buzzing sound. It was his Tomato Can, strapped to his leg inside its water tight, coffin-like box.

Angel . . .

"I thought you were going to call me?" she asked him on answering the phone.

He started to explain it all to her, near-euphoria creeping into his voice—when something else caught his attention. He told her he was all right and that he loved her but he had to call her right back.

He was distracted by a man stretched out on a nearby beach lounge chair, waving to him. The man had huge dark sunglasses on and was wearing an unacceptably tiny Speedo. With an enormous drink in one hand, he was beckoning to him with the other.

Starr froze on the spot.

Yes, strange things had happened to him all his life—mind-bending coincidences, episodes of extreme precognition, hearing the voices of the dead.

But what he thought he was seeing now just couldn't possibly be.

Yet it was.

The man was now laughing and aggressively waving him over, pointing to his enormous drink and inviting him to have one.

"O . . . M . . . G," Starr actually heard himself say out loud.

It was Boris.

"But how?" Starr asked him, astonished. "How did you possibly survive?"

Boris shrugged and with a laugh said simply: "I swim."

The tale that was later told was Dima Gurtovoy and the rest of his crew was lost at sea when the An-225B crashed off the Skeleton Coast, a watery graveyard for many aircraft.

Searches proved fruitless. End of story.

For Moscow, that was one big problem solved.

But this cover story allowed everyone involved to start a new life. No longer on the Kremlin's radar, Dima,

Minky and Misha were quietly given U.S. citizenship. Boris, Oleg and Stan chose to stay in the U.S. as well. Dima had promised to set them up with new lives, new identities and new jobs, plus when the time was right they would quietly contact their families and have them brought over too. In the end, they would all wind up working for the New York Knicks basketball team, which Dima would go on to purchase via a shell company leaving the tale of him losing his life at sea in a plane crash intact.

As for the wreckage of the An-225B, the sands of the Skeleton Coast covered it completely within two days of the crash. It would not be uncovered again for many, many years.

They took Misha to the resort's medical office who in turn made arrangements to have her airlifted out and brought to the hospital in Windhoek in Namibia. This done, the other survivors re-united with Boris, they too astonished he was still alive, and joined him on lounge chairs for food and drinks.

Starr had another, much longer conversation with Angel, this time using a burner phone bought at the resort. Once she was convinced he was truly okay, they both agreed it was probably for the best that they hadn't connected with ONI headquarters, spilling the beans about the Tomato Can.

Incredibly, for the moment anyway, their secret was still safe.

After contacting ONI himself, during which they promised to secure air transport out for all of the survivors the next morning, Starr joined the others down by the water's edge, intent on sucking down as many drinks as he could before inevitably falling asleep.

He was three drinks into this plan when he heard that familiar sound coming from his ankle pocket.

It was the Tomato Can again.

But who was this? He and Angel had just agreed not to use the obsolete sat-phone at least until they could discuss it in person.

Why then was she calling him on it now?

He walked away from the others and hit the receive button.

But it wasn't Angel.

It was the other woman, her ethereal voice calling his name.

And finally he was able to answer: "Yes, who is this?"

And finally she responded.

"It's Maura," he heard her say. "And I just had to tell you that I've been seeing monks lately in the strangest places . . ."

Part Three

The God Satellite

Chapter One

Near Ghost Creek, Arizona
Two weeks later

It was another, typical night atop Mount Graham.

Just above freezing, wind gusts up to 30 knots, snow squalls off and on.

The six-man security team watching over the observatory were in their dugouts, out of the weather but keeping an eye on things. Basically a big hole in the ground, expertly camouflaged and made rustically livable inside, these ODs were positioned in a semi-circle around the building's parking lot, providing a wide field of view. Each man was equipped with a NVG-T helmet, giving them the ability to see at night with both night-vision and, by utilizing an adjustable monocle, thermal, infra-red images.

Once an hour, one security man would emerge from his hole and walk the property, inspecting all doors and windows as well as checking the dozen motion detectors and video cams hidden around the perimeter. Sometimes the wind or small animals would trip these devices and the patrolling guard would have to reset them.

This was what the security team's second in command was doing just around midnight.

A motion detector on the northern edge of the parking lot had been tripped by the wind. He re-set it and then called the team chief in his slightly larger command OD so he could reacquire the device's signal on his smart phone.

But the team chief did not reply.

The man tried the call again; still nothing. There was always a chance the chief had dozed off, but that was not likely. Everyone on the security team was highly regarded and ex-special ops; falling asleep on the job just wasn't in their DNA.

He called the next senior guy, but he didn't answer either. From the northern corner of the property, and by cranking up his thermal-imaging monocle, the guard could see this man's OD. As expertly hidden as it was, he knew its location because he'd helped to build it.

When the third guy he called didn't answer either, the guard's concern grew. This was hardly typical. He'd talked to these people just minutes before—where the hell were they?

When four and five didn't answer either, the guard knew something was seriously wrong. Clicking the safety off his AR-15, he left the motion detector station, hurried across the parking lot and into the woods, arriving at the nearest OD, the one he'd helped dig. He found his colleague inside, unconscious and face down, bleeding from the ears.

There were no signs of trauma or struggle, but the air had a heavy disinfectant-type smell.

Damn . . .

Chloroform . . .

The man reached for his gas mask, but it wasn't on his utility belt; he'd left it back in his own OD. Holding his nose, he scrambled out of the hole, stumbling twice before getting to his feet. Someone was inside the wire; he had to warn the observatory.

But before he could raise his cell phone, his NVG-T helmet warmed up and he realized a person was standing in the woods just a few feet in front of him. It was a nun. She looked otherworldly in the emerald world of night vision, her habit blowing in the wind. This was supremely odd. There were a couple dozen nuns assigned to the observatory, but they never left the building.

"Why are you out here, sister?" he asked her, totally perplexed. "You should be inside with the others."

"Just breathe deep," she replied.

In the next second, someone grabbed him from behind and put a rag over his nose and mouth. It too smelled like disinfectant.

He chose to struggle, but it didn't last long. At his first sign of resistance, the nun punched him so hard on the jaw it felt like he'd been hit by a pair of brass knuckles. He went to the ground head first, his NVG-T helmet bouncing away into the trees.

Eyesight wavy, consciousness failing, he looked up to see the nun standing directly over him. And now a monk had joined her.

"You shouldn't be out here," was all he could say to them before everything went black.

The Graham Observatory did not operate on Mountain Standard Time.

It ran on the same time as Rome, Italy, eight hours ahead. This meant midnight was morning for those inside the plain-white, square building.

The place did not have a cafeteria; it had a small kitchen instead. Employees ate at their desks or work stations, their meals delivered courtesy of the Vatican-supplied service staff. In the case of breakfast, all meals would usually be delivered before the stroke of twelve.

It was shortly after midnight now. Normally the observatory's small kitchen staff would have rolled out their several dozen movable trays by now, delivering the morning meal.

When this had not happened by 12:15, two technicians made their way to the kitchen to find a puzzling sight. There was a traffic jam of food carts just inside the swinging doors; most contained hot meals, one was simply holding a cup of tea, all of them assigned with room numbers. But there was no sign of the two-person staff.

The technicians discovered the back door to the observatory slightly ajar. Beyond was the building's loading dock and dumpster. The kitchen staff—a Benedictine monk and nun—were laid out and unconscious on the loading dock. There was a strong odor of disinfectant around them and on their clothes.

The startled technicians tried to revive the pair, but both were out cold. Attempting to seek further help, they tried to get back into the kitchen only to find the door was now locked behind them, stranding them outside.

Security footage would later show, just as the general alarm was sounding inside the observatory, a monk and a nun were seen moving out of the kitchen and walking quickly towards the main concourse of the building. But as soon as the alert was raised, every hallway on every floor was suddenly crowded with monks and nuns, hurrying in all directions. The two targets were lost in the chaos.

It was a loop of three warning klaxons blasting throughout the observatory. Three blasts meant two things. Unauthorized persons were inside the building and while security teams were trying to find them, all employees should shelter in place.

Admiral Millflower was in the observatory's chapel when the alarms went off.

She was not praying; she was texting. She didn't care for breakfast at midnight, so while others indulged, she came here to use her cell phone for private communications, usually asking only for a cup of tea to be brought to her. That was another odd thing about the observatory. The place was run by the Vatican, yet its chapel was not used very much. It was a good place to hide.

She was instantly anxious at the first sound of the klaxon though. Her side arm was back at her office and no one but the kitchen staff knew she was here. Sheltering in place, unarmed, in the face of some unknown threat, was suddenly a very unnerving proposition. She knew the security cams and the motion detectors outside were going off all the time. But never had anyone unauthorized actually gotten inside the building—or had even tried to.

A nun appeared from behind the curtains of the sacristy on her right. Hurrying along with the warning klaxon, she began extinguishing all the candles on the small altar. In seconds, the already subdued chapel was almost completely dark.

That's when Millflower realized someone else was in the chapel with her. Suddenly a Benedictine monk was sitting in the pew right next to her, appearing as if out of nowhere.

A pro, she thought.

The monk pulled back his hood just enough to reveal himself. She gasped a little on seeing his face.

It was Chris Starr.

This truly surprised her. Of all the people involved in this thing, she never thought he would be the first one to actually figure it out.

"Sorry, Admiral," he said to her, gently taking away her cell phone, at the same time showing her he was armed. "But I need a few answers from you."

When he finally got back to San Diego, Starr fulfilled his dream of having an Irish beer with Angel while sitting at her kitchen table.

After a 24-hour aerial odyssey that featured stops in Botswana, the Azores, Jamaica and for some reason, Tulsa, Oklahoma, he still had sand in his hair, in his ears and in his boots—but no matter. They had four beers each, after which he staggered into her bedroom, collapsed and went to sleep.

But he was up early the next morning, talking to Maura on his Tomato Can.

She told him how she saw monks standing in the shadows of her hometown pub the previous Saturday night and again in the last pew of her parish church the following day. On both occasions she couldn't see their faces, but they seemed to be staring right at her, only for her to blink and find them gone.

Though convinced she was going mad, at the same time, she felt that by their very presence, hallucination or not, someone was trying to tell her something. That's why she reached out to Starr.

He then told her about his own otherworldly monk sighting. Hopelessly lost in the desert, standing on the top of that dune, thick fog all around. And how, strange as it seemed, the vision might have saved his life.

The whole thing was creepy and outlandish. But it was also clear that something very peculiar was happening . . . to both of them.

After a little discussion, they came to wonder if the visions were connected to their first visit to the observatory. They knew the place employed monks—and nuns too. They saw some there that first time. Why else then would they be imagining these friar types?

Maybe when they'd had their retinas scanned before leaving the observatory that time, something was partially erased from their memories—but not completely. Maybe because their two minds were entwined more than they'd ever imagined, cerebral artifacts like seeing monks lingered when everything had been washed away. So, maybe, they'd been duped somehow by Admiral Millflower.

Or maybe they were both simply going crazy.

Whatever the case, they agreed they had to find out.

What was happening now, here inside the observatory, was all Maura's idea. Dressing in the religious habits, employing the chloroform, sneaking into the kitchen, finding out where Admiral Millflower was at that moment (the lone tea cup giving her away), and then accosting her—it was all part of a grand scheme she'd dreamed up while flying back to the U.S. from Dublin.

"We've already broken into a monastery," was how she explained it to him. "This will be nothing."

***

The Admiral never stopped staring at him, her pretty features still drooped in disbelief. But while she was greatly mystified seeing him here, dressed like this, she almost laughed when he showed her his weapon.

244

"What are you going to do if I don't talk?" she asked him now. "Do you really think that I'll think you'll shoot me here—shoot me dead? Because that's what it's going to take."

But Starr just waved her off. He pulled out his burner phone and opened it to a locked file containing an extensive expense sheet from ONI's accounting division. It documented Millflower making numerous trips to Italy in the days leading up to Father Friendly's last mission, something she failed to mention to them.

"Just from this alone," Starr told her, "we can prove you were lying to us from the very beginning about this thing. And not for any reasons we can find having to do with National Security."

"What can I say?" she replied blithely. "I love Italy—and I admit it was a misappropriation of funds. But still, it's a slap on the wrist."

Starr then produced an image taken from a security camera showing Millflower leaving her hotel in Rome, wholly out of uniform. Instead she was wearing black leather head to toe.

She studied the image and then just shrugged. "So, okay, I bought some off-market clothes while I was there. You caught me."

Another image showed her entering a very subdued looking establishment in downtown Naples, a place that resembled a club *prive.*

Another shrug. "I took in some of the sights," she said dryly.

She looked back at Starr and finally smiled.

"I admire your pluck, Lieutenant Commander," she said. "And how you managed to get back in here should be studied by our people, because obviously there's a flaw in the security system. But what's actually happening here is beyond you. It's beyond me. It's something so strange that just about anyone involved in it will be absolved of all their sins, shall we say, simply because of their connection to it."

She actually touched his knee and started to say: "So, my advice to you is . . ." when suddenly the top of the wooden pew where she was seated shattered not an inch from her left shoulder. An instant later, another piece of the pew, this one off her right shoulder, also exploded, sending a mini-storm of splinters off in all directions.

They both looked up to see Maura, face exposed but still in full nun attire, aiming her Glock at the Admiral's forehead. It had a silencer attached to it now; the device was almost as long as the pistol's barrel itself.

And it had worked amazingly well. Silencers in real life weren't like those seen in the movies. The real ones made noise, more like a muffled pop, but were never completely silent. But Maura's weapon was very quiet, emitting only the slightest puffing sound.

Still, it startled the Admiral so much, she put her hands up in front of her face in the classic defensive posture.

"You're right," Starr told her. "I wouldn't shoot you. But I can't say the same for my partner. Luckily, she's a good shot."

Maura took two more steps closer to her.

"But that's the funny thing." she said, somewhat menacingly. "I'm a pretty lousy shot actually. I don't know where the next bullet might be going . . ."

The Admiral kept her hands up until Starr reached over and calmly pulled them back down.

But still, Maura continued to snarl at her. "So, at the very least you were meeting Father Friendly in sex clubs," she said. "I just hope the reason you did this was related to something relevant in this matter. Because if not, hooking up with a man of the cloth at a swingers bar is wrong on so many levels."

Millflower scoffed again. "Said the nun holding the gun on me . . ."

Starr jumped in at this point.

"If the whole Father Friendly winning money thing was basically a trial run of your magnificent satellite," he asked, "Why did the money go to Belfast war victims? That war was over a long time ago. Why not victims of a more recent war? Or something closer to home?"

"Or something a little less dangerous," Maura added angrily. "Something that doesn't involve gangsters and terrorists and unpleasant truck bombs?"

The Admiral was immediately both crestfallen and surprised.

"*That's* what you want to know?" she gasped back. "Of everything involved in this thing, that's it?"

Both Starr and Maura nodded.

"Because it's just the one thing that might lead into so many other things," Starr told her. "I also got access to your expense account records for the past two years, in places where you served. Yet there were no corresponding expenditures anywhere in those two years which would indicate any kind of U.S. military-Vatican connection."

"So?" she asked defiantly.

"So, if you're not here on official Navy business," Starr shot back. "Why are you here?"

Millflower just shook her head. "I know it sounds like a bad James Bond movie," she replied, almost wistfully. "But like I just tried to explain to you, this goes beyond NILE or ONI. It goes beyond the entire United States military, the entire government. And for the record, I was asked to come here. And I'm honored to say it."

"Even though it appears like you've violated just about every security protocol in the book?" Maura fired at her.

Millflower just shook her head and looked back at Starr. "Can you remind me again how the Irish Police got involved in this?"

This infuriated Maura. She took a step closer to Millflower, the long silencer now just a few inches from the Admiral's head.

But Starr all but ignored this, concentrating instead on the klaxons still wailing around the building.

"There's no time for that," he told Millflower, getting her to her feet. "You've got to bring us there, right now . . ."

"And where's 'there?' " the Admiral asked.

Suddenly, the Glock silencer was resting between the Admiral's manicured eyebrows.

"You know where," Maura growled at her.

Chapter Two

On Starr's insistence, Millflower cancelled the observatory's security alert.

Plugging into the building's PA system from her cellphone in the chapel, she declared the emergency a false alarm and asked all employees to return to their stations, including the security personnel.

Then Starr put his hood up, Maura let her veils down and placing the Admiral between them, they left the chapel and started walking.

They were soon in a part of the building they hadn't seen before. It was a long, curving hallway and although it had offices on both sides, it was like being in a church. Thick carpet, subdued lighting, flickering votive candles stuck in alcoves and next to doorways everywhere. The smell of incense was in the air.

Everything but Renaissance murals on the ceiling.

They kept walking, trying to look like they knew what they were doing, the Admiral playing her part. They passed many monks and nuns along the way. Always in pairs, heads-down, they were devotedly hurrying about, doing who knew what.

They came to an elevator with a sign next to the buttons that read: "Visitors: Observation Room is on 1st Level."

It was here for the first time they saw an unusual image. A decal on the elevator door depicted a simple medieval painting showing two men riding on one horse.

"That's an emblem of the Knights Templar," Maura whispered to Starr.

"Those guys again," he replied.

According to 6th Fleet HQ's intelligence officer, while recovering from his head injury at Ramstein, Father Friendly told doctors he'd come to believe he was a reincarnated member of the Knights Templar of the Da Vinci Code fame.

Now this . . .

But what did one have to do with the other?

They went down five floors, silently, finally arriving in the observatory's sub-basement. The elevator opened into another hallway where they found two massive wooden doors facing them, doors one might see in a church. A more formal sign above them read: "Observation Room" and again it was accompanied by the image of two men riding a horse.

With the Admiral in the lead, they walked through the doors.

As they'd seen before, the Observation Room was a large, wide open space that looked like a re-creation of NASA's Mission Control—but obviously that time they were watching not a live feed from the place, but a pre-recorded video to fool them into thinking this was just an ordinary, if out of the way, satellite tracking station.

In reality, the Observation Room looked like the set of a super-strange science fiction movie. Monks were sitting behind the rows of monitoring screens instead of the space program-type engineers. There was no smoking, no coffee—and no one was hurrying around. The place was absolutely quiet. Again, just like in a church.

Above them was the observatory's telescope. Lit by dozens of small yellow-halogen lights, it seemed like it was made of gold. Below it was a great white parabolic dish, at least 30 feet across and sparkling to the point of dazzling. Starr recognized it as a satellite relay antenna.

But it was the real Observation Room itself that held him most in awe. It had a panoramic wrap-around video screen that showed a 360-degree image of the Earth, apparently shot and pieced together by many different cameras in orbit.

And front and center of this extravagant display was an enormous, very bizarre-looking spacecraft.

At least 100 feet long and somewhat tubular—it looked nothing like the satellite they'd seen in the fake pre-taped view of this place. This thing resembled a giant-sized medieval chalice with a cup at both ends. More like a work of art than something scientific, it was green and gold and turning slowly, revealing many curves and soft angles in its design. Hundreds of tiny blinking lights were imbedded all over it, giving it a Christmas tree look. And it was pointed straight at the Earth.

The God Satellite . . .

The *real* one . . .

The high strangeness didn't end there. The silent monks sitting at their monitoring stations were odd enough, but what was on their read-out screens was truly weird. Just like at NASA, these monitors were filled with lines of data. But the numbers were displayed in Roman numerals and the attending text was being transmitted in Latin.

Starr turned his attention back to the satellite. It looked so . . . anachronistic. Out of date. Just plain old. He couldn't imagine any modern space program designing and launching anything so odd looking.

By this time, the satellite had turned to a point where he could see something embossed on the side.

It read: *Maius II MDXIX.*

He nudged Maura. "May 2nd?" he whispered. "In the year, 1519?"

"Oh my God," she said under her breath. "That's Leonardo Da Vinci's birthday . . ."

They were without words for another few seconds. But Maura was fighting to contain herself.

"This is extremely disturbing," she finally said. "And while I don't know what this place is, nothing here looks 'American' to me. It appears all-Vatican."

Starr agreed.

And so did the Admiral.

"We in the military have known about this satellite for just a little while," she told them in a hushed voice. "But certain people in the United States' government and selected people around the world have been aware of it for a long, long time now."

"What's a long, long time?" Maura asked her. "The first satellite was put up by the Russians in 1957, so . . ."

Her voice trailed off when she saw the Admiral slowly shaking her head.

"The Russians were not the first to put something in orbit," she replied softly. "That's one of the top five secrets in the world. And when I say certain people in the U.S. government have known about this satellite's existence for a long time, I mean, a *long* time. As in all the way back to the Lincoln Administration."

Starr and Maura's jaws dropped on cue.

"But . . . how?" Starr asked.

"We don't know," the Admiral replied. "Supposedly it was first spotted by the Royal Observatory in Greenwich, England back in 1680. They didn't know what it was but they knew it was different from the stars or the planets or anything else up there. The British government managed to keep its existence secret and then passed it on to the United States just before the Civil War."

She nodded towards the mysterious satellite on the huge video screen.

"I mean, look at it," she said. "It's certainly not of a modern design. And the fact that it has Leonardo Da Vinci's birthdate on it might give us a clue when it was built. But how it got up there—we have no idea."

"Then what is all this?" Starr asked indicating the Observation Room.

The Admiral chose her next words carefully.

"Over the years, some learned people, working in secret, and financed by some of the wealthiest families in the world, tried to make contact with the satellite," she told them. "Millions were spent on this, but most of it in failure.

"But only just recently, we've been able to activate it and work with it. Before all this, it's just been floating around up there, somnambulant. And that activation only happened because someone discovered the satellite responds only to special radio frequencies, way up on the spectrum.

"And besides this place, the only way to communicate with it is through that old Navy satellite phone, the one you gave me—or I should say, returned to me—when we first met."

Starr suddenly felt very uneasy. They'd theorized that the observatory was a front for leaking secret information to some of America's adversaries, or maybe a place where illegal eavesdropping—on Americans or someone else—was taking place.

But this . . . this was almost beyond comprehension.

"But why are you suddenly telling us all this?" he asked the Admiral.

She didn't reply right away. Instead, she nodded to someone they couldn't see and suddenly the low-lit lights in the Observation Room went out completely, only to be replaced with another kind of light. Luminous, sparkling everywhere, dazzling.

Only then did she say: "Maybe you should ask someone else . . ."

Starr and Maura turned towards the light and saw something that was indeed . . . incomprehensible.

Standing just behind them was a man wearing a monk's habit. But the sparkling lights all around made him look surreal and very different from the other monks nearby. His presence was puzzling.

"Why this person?" Starr asked the Admiral.

She smiled broadly. "Because they have the answers to all of your questions," she said. "In fact, they've had them all along."

That's when the monk pulled his hood down and for the first time they could see his face.

Starr was so startled he felt like a bolt of electricity had gone through him. Maura grabbed his hand again and this time stuck her fingernails into him deep.

They just couldn't believe it.

It was Father Friendly.

"Good to see the both of you again," he told them with a smile. Then he revealed he had a small, almost-antique Instamatic flash camera in his hands.

He pointed it at them and said: "Now, please, just for a moment . . . smile . . ."

Flash!

Chapter Three

Starr woke up to someone gently slapping his face.

He opened his eyes to see a man dressed in firefighter gear trying to revive him.

"What the hell . . .?"

"You're okay," the guy was saying to him. "Just a bump on the head."

He was in the front seat of their Hyundai rental, but the car was in a ditch near the bottom of the Mount Graham fire road.

Looking out the cracked windshield, he saw Maura standing up on the road with other first responders, wrapped in a blanket, but looking uninjured.

Against his rescuer's wishes, he climbed out of the car himself and scrambled out of the ditch to join Maura. She hugged him tightly.

"Don't let go," she kept saying. "Please, just a little longer."

The silent flashing lights of the rescue vehicles added more weirdness to the already eerie situation.

Two paramedics appeared. Only then did they finally disentangle themselves.

"Do you remember what happened?" one medic asked them.

Maura turned to Starr. "Do you remember it?" she asked him, almost in tears now.

He shook away the cobwebs.

"Yes," he said. "But tell me again . . ."

"I think we were inside . . . a spaceship?" she said. "A UFO? Were we . . . my God, were we abducted?"

Starr's head was pounding; it was almost a hangover type of headache. But in between the throbs, something in the back of his mind was thinking the same thing. They'd been inside a craft of some kind with lots of bright lights in their eyes and shadowy hooded shapes around them.

"You might be right," he finally managed to say, not quite believing his own words.

"Do you want us to put that in our report?" the other paramedic asked them.

Before they could answer, an Arizona State Police cruiser arrived, an ambulance right behind it.

Without another word, two state troopers escorted Maura to the ambulance and put her in the back. She only had enough time to wave goodbye through the vehicle's rear window then she was gone.

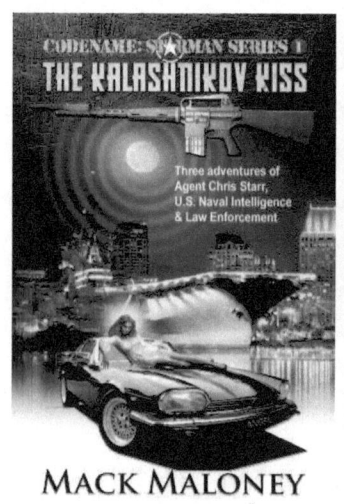

On Sale Now!
MACK MALONEY

**"The best high-action thriller writer
out there today, bar none."
—Jon Land, *USA Today* bestselling author**

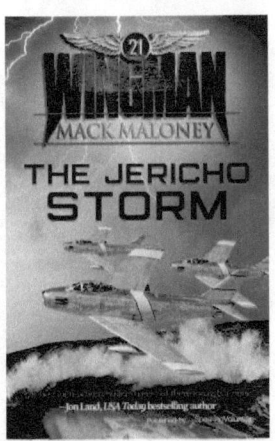

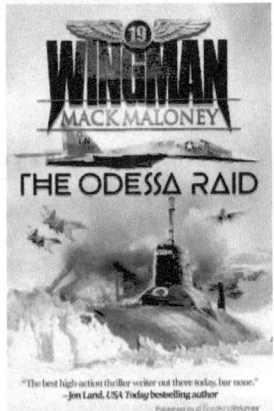

For more information
visit: www.SpeakingVolumes.us

 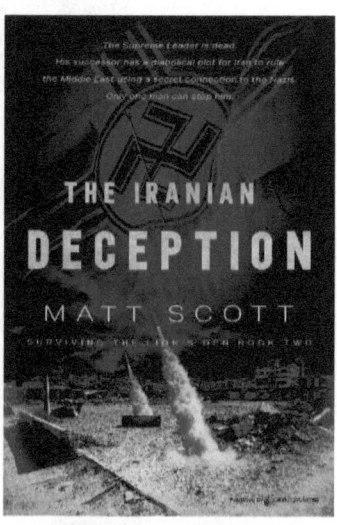

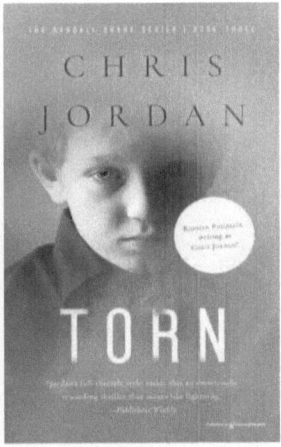
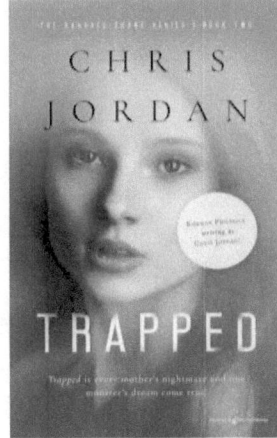
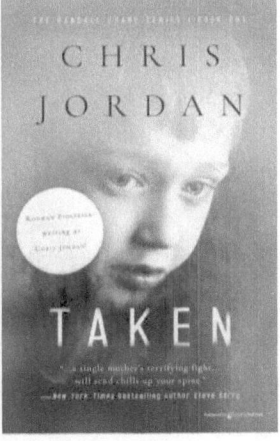